S

First Love
&
Look for
My Obituary

Two Novellas
by

ELENA GARRO

translated by David Unger

CURBSTONE PRESS

FIRST EDITION, 1997
Copyright © 1997 by Elena Garro
Translation Copyright © 1997 by David Unger
All Rights Reserved

Printed in Canada on acid-free paper by Best Book Manufacturers
Cover illustration: "Chrysis, 1967", Paul Delvaux
                    reprinted with permission of Ediciones Castillo

David Unger would like to thank Hardie St. Martin for his suggestions
on the translation.

The publisher thanks Jane Blanshard and Barbara Rosen for their
editorial help.

This book was published with the support of the
Connecticut Commission on the Arts and the National
Endowment for the Arts, and donations from many
individuals.We are very grateful for this support.

Library of Congress Cataloging-in-Publication Data

    Garro, Elena.
        [Primer amor. English]
        First love; & Look for my obituary : two novellas / by Elena
    Garro; [translated by David Unger]. — 1st ed.
            p.   cm.
        ISBN 1-880684-51-9
        1. Garro, Elena—Translations into English. I. Unger, David.
        II. Garro, Elena. Busca mi esquela. English. III. Title.
        IV. Look for my obituary.
    PQ7297.G3585A28   1997
    863—dc21   97-23521

published by
CURBSTONE PRESS   321 Jackson Street   Willimantic, CT 06226
        phone: (860) 423-5110   e-mail: curbston@connix.com
                http://www.connix.com/~curbston/

Sor Juana Inés de la Cruz Prize
1996

TWO NOVELLAS

First Love

&

Look for My Obituary

FIRST LOVE

"THERE ARE ALWAYS men in train aisles," thought Barbara, as a man offered to help her cross from one car to the next. Her mother, the other Barbara, nodded to express her thanks, but refused the outstretched hand. In the dining car, Barbara noticed how the same man sat at the next table and observed the way her mother ate a pear as yellow as an autumn leaf. Later, when she raced back and forth down the aisle, he stopped her and asked, somewhat indiscreetly: "Why is your sister so sad?"

Barbara said nothing. She felt so unsure of herself. Why did her mother wear moccasins and smoke one cigarette after another? Other mothers were fat and wore dark brown hats. She went back to their compartment without answering him and picked up the book where Viking queens gave orders with a flick of the wrist to golden-haired princes. The noise of her mother's gold bracelets as she lit each cigarette made her lift her eyes and observe her hunched over a book. "She is sad" the young girl said to herself, gazing at her blond straight hair as it slid down to her shoulders.

Barbara had a secret she could not share with the man in the aisle: her mother was always sad. At home, she watched her walk aimlessly through the drafty rooms. She saw her image reflected in all the mirrors, indifferent to what was going on about her. Every afternoon the two of them drank hot tea and read in the yellow-painted room. They went to bed early and spoke very little. No one had ever breathed a word of it, but she knew that her father did not love her mother. "He doesn't love her," and she seemed surprised time and again by this always new revelation. One Sunday she found herself sitting across from her father in *Au Diable Rose,* a black market tearoom. It was a rose-colored room and a heavily scented woman came over and offered them cookies and hot chocolate. Barbara felt that this quiet place, which was like a heart filled with unexpected fragrances, caressed her. There you could only find pastries and beautiful, barely whispered words.

She looked admiringly at her father. He leaned over and let his light-colored eyes rest on her for a minute: "Barbara, when you grow up, try not to be like her; that would be disastrous for me."

His words fell like stones into her tiny cup of hot chocolate. She was surprised that the cup didn't shatter to pieces. Her father's eyes went on watching her for a while.

"I won't be like her," she promised, scared as she was.

"We're opposites. You should be more Mediterranean, like me," her father ordered.

Barbara did not understand. She glanced at him curiously, no longer wanting to drink her chocolate.

"Mediterranean?" she repeated.

"The barbarians are from the north which represents hypocrisy, puritanism, cruelty. Just don't grow up to be like that mad woman..."

She returned home scared out of her wits. That evening she saw them going out together. Her mother leaned over the bed to kiss her; her saffron outfit, her blond hair, her gold bracelets made her resemble one of the barbarian queens in the stories her mother had given her. She felt frightened. Behind her mother stood her father, with his dark hair and skin; he seemed fragile and that worried her. They had barely walked out of the room when Barbara looked at herself in the mirror above the chimney. Why had he asked me not to be like her?

Now on the train the same nagging question kept her from reading; her eyes lingered on her mother, bent over her book. She noticed her plaid skirt and moccasins and worriedly returned to the image of the Viking queen who was alive in the pages of her book. At dusk they reached the seashore. No one was waiting for them at the station. No one ever waited for them anywhere. Barbara picked up the suitcases and started walking with deliberate steps. They walked for a few minutes in silence. The station was on the outskirts of town. A cold wind was blowing.

"Are you sad, Barbara?"

Her mother turned around to look at her.

"Me, sad? Don't ever say that. A general is never sad; sure, there are moments when he weeps over his losses..." she answered, slowing her steps.

In the hotel a woman with closely cropped hair took them to their room. She was the owner, spoke gruffly, and had red, splotchy hands. The room was enormous, with a huge bed and a window that faced the rear of a church tower. The window smelled of plant growth. Beyond the tower, a scented breeze blew in from the green hills.

"We'll have dinner here," her mother decided.

There was a mirror in the room and while the mother looked out on the balcony, the young girl, seated on a suitcase, watched her mother's image reflected in the mirror: solitude and sadness flew like loose threads from her shoulders and her unruffled hair.

"We're going for a long walk tomorrow," her mother said, as if promising her a prize.

Barbara did not answer. She was used to long walks. Her mother loved nothing more than going on long walks.

The following morning they were both awakened by the clucking of hens; they jumped out of bed, gladdened by the clear sky and the cackling. They went out to explore the town.

They found themselves in a cobblestoned, triangular square, facing the church and the bakery. Barbara dug out their ration coupons and purchased a piece of bread which she filled with chocolate bars they had brought from America. They started walking till they found themselves, a few minutes later, in the countryside. Seven strange men were walking in front of them. They all had light skin, overgrown hair; and a few of tufts had turned almost white because of the sun. They were wearing torn green rags for clothes. A huge white P stood out on their backs. All seven carried shovels and pickaxes on their shoulders. Mother and daughter walked behind them for a while. Then they stopped, looked around, and bent down to work on the broken road.

"They're German prisoners," said Barbara.

As she passed them, she smiled and said: "*Güten mörgen.*"

The men stood straight up and glared; they formed a circle around them and began talking in German as if moved by the same impulse.

"No, we're not Germans," Barbara explained.

The men looked at one another and began laughing. One of them leaned over to the younger Barbara, took her in his arms and lifted her up to the sky, examining her with his blue, curious eyes. The girl glanced at his sunburnt skin and straggly hair; she felt magnetically attracted to the man holding her in the air and looking at her with eyes shining and wet like drops of water. When he put her back on the ground, she saw his toes sticking through ragged boots; she suddenly became sad. The man squatted next to her.

"What's your name?" he asked in a foreign accent.

"Barbara...And what's yours?"

The men broke into laughter and began talking in voices deep as bass drums just above her.

"Well, I'm Siegfried," answered the squatting man.

Her mother sat on a rock and offered them cigarettes. The seven young men looked at one another in surprise and accepted them cheerfully.

"When are you going back to Germany?" Barbara asked, looking at each and every one of them, surprised that they were so young.

"We'll go on working here until the fate of the prisoners is decided," one of them answered softly. The others said nothing. They suddenly seemed so sad. The young girl felt that, just like her mother, nobody wanted them and without knowing why she also grew somber.

"We're not supposed to talk to anyone. If they see you with us, they'll give you a hard time," said Siegfried, looking at Barbara with eyes so blue they resembled a gleaming streak of sky.

The young woman contemptuously shrugged her shoulders.

"I'll do whatever I want," she answered softly.

They remained like that for a long while, not talking. The prisoners were caught off balance by the sudden friendship of the girl and the young woman who offered them cigarettes, while the mother and daughter were surprised by the youth and wretched condition of the prisoners.

"Is the beach far off?" asked Barbara, embarrassed, realizing that the prisoners weren't going there.

The circle of men broke to show her the way to the sea.

They all seemed willing to take her to it just to please her. Yes, it was far off, but they were opening a shortcut to the beach through the cliffs. They were about to show them the way, but they pulled up short and looked at her helplessly. Siegfried whacked an open hand with a closed fist, stuck both hands into the pockets of his ripped jacket and stared stubbornly at the ground. Barbara realized they could not abandon their forced labor without risking a punishment she could not forestall.

"It doesn't matter. I'll find it on my own," she said cheerfully.

They said goodbye to one another; before going, Barbara took out her American cigarettes and held them out to the prisoners. The circle of young men blushed; she then took a step toward Siegfried and placed the pack in his jacket pocket. Instinctively, the soldier took the woman's soft hand, held it in his and looked into her eyes with longing in spite of himself.

"Please keep them," she begged.

The soldier said nothing; he stared at her entranced. The other soldiers either lowered their eyes or else looked at the sky, respectful of the confusion that the young woman—dressed in navy blue shorts and top, with blond hair blowing in the wind and shapely as a seashell—had produced on their companion. Her presence, her nearness, too, made them recall the days when they were free, the years with their families, and they grew somber: prisoners in shame, cut off from the love-filled daily lives of the people all around them.

Heads lowered, Barbara and her daughter trod off, watched by the seven men whose eyes followed them in wonder until they merged with the green hills. They just walked around in a fog for a few hours, with no desire to go to the beach. Green herbs scented the morning and opened sudden inroads into the sky's silvery air. They walked past groups of red-roofed houses and stopped to watch the peasants leading teams of oxen, letting their grunts echo on the hillsides.

"Are they soldiers?" the younger Barbara asked.

"Yes...'Offer a silver bridge to a fleeing enemy,'" Barbara answered grudgingly.

The seven tattered blond young men had shattered the morning's harmony. The balance of beauty in the sunlight contradicted the humiliation inflicted on the seven soldiers splitting rocks. They were Germans and therefore did not deserve anyone's respect or pity; they had been beaten and even their last remaining dignity had to be broken. Their very presence indicated a failure on the part of the victors.

They passed the prisoners on their way back. The seven stood in a line at the side of the road and waved, saying "*Auf wiedersehen!*"

From her tiny frame, Barbara sought out Siegfried's eyes as they glanced at her mother. Later, in the hotel dining room, she asked: "Where are they now?"

"Splitting rocks," she answered evenly.

The hotel guests were staring at them. Almost all the young people were dressed in white and wore silk ascots around their throats. Their bright eyes and hair contrasted with the tousled blond hair of the prisoners. Barbara was set on not looking at anyone and she ordered her daughter not to raise her eyes from her plate.

They went out to have coffee on the terrace under the shadow of the arbor, on a table off to the side.

"If you want sugar in your coffee it'll cost 50 francs for each cube."

Barbara ordered lots of cubes and dunked them in her mother's coffee; while she was chewing on one, she once more thought of the German prisoners.

"Where are they now?" she asked again.

"Splitting rocks!" her mother answered calmly.

The hotel owner walked over stealthily.

"Madame, I've been told that you spoke to the Germans."

Barbara raised her eyes and stared at him in astonishment.

"I beg you not to do that again."

Barbara did not answer. She didn't like orders, especially if they ran against her desires or her principles. From a nearby table, two dark young men watched the exchange.

"Let's go to our room," said Barbara to her daughter. She stood up and took the young girl's hand.

When they got upstairs, she opened the suitcase where she stored the sweets she had brought from America: she took out chocolate drops, packets of cookies and cigarettes. She dropped them in the beach bag, next to their bathing suits and headed, holding her daughter's hand, to where the prisoners were. From far off they saw them splitting rocks, bent under a three o'clock sun.

Barbara had the feeling that the young men were not surprised by their visit. Her mother sat calmly on a rock and the men stopped working to observe them carefully. They watched them arrive, despite their exhaustion which had developed long before their present work detail—as if they had endured horrible days that were etched in their eyes. Siegfried blushed and took a step toward them.

"Have you eaten?" asked Barbara, trying to adopt an indifferent tone.

"We eat at six...in the prison," the young man answered with dignity.

Barbara avoided looking at them. She opened her white canvas bag and took out the chocolates and cookies.

"We came to have dessert with you," she said, handing them the sweets.

The young Germans squatted around the two Barbaras and ate their cookies and chocolates without lifting their eyes. Siegfried put an arm around the young girl and pulled her close to him. Barbara noticed that he would not look into her daughter's eyes. Klaus began talking about Hamburg and about his brothers. He'd had no news of them. The others also had no idea what had happened to their families. They were simply there, waiting in frozen time, cut off from life and from emotions, for nations to decide their fate...

Manfred brushed off the blond, scraggly curls that fell over his eyes. "My mother and two sisters were burned alive in the bombing of Dresden. The world will never be the same again."

From that day on, Barbara and her daughter would pass by the Germans, either on their way to the beach or heading back to their hotel. They'd always stop and talk a while with them. The men knew exactly when their friends would be passing and would wait for them, their eyes searching the green path running between the rocks and the hills. Sometimes, as the sun was setting, mother and daughter would linger with the soldiers and come back with them part of the way to town. It wouldn't be prudent to be seen returning together. The prisoners would wait on the side of the road, while the two of them continued alone back to the hotel. Almost always, Siegfried would stand next to the mother and admire her profile with lowered eyes. Barbara would also watch him. He was maybe twenty years old. His shoulders still had a kind of teenage vulnerability, and when he turned his head, he seemed a mere boy. His large hands and wide palms were not yet those of a man. His sadness, which contrasted with the beauty of the hills, made the hills seem guilty of the fate of that young, defenseless boy cut off from love. These were lifeless days for the seven young men, surrounded only by the stupid hostility of the other people.

"The nights are even sadder than the days," said Siegfried glancing down.

Barbara looked at him sadly. She had never even considered what the nights must be like for these young men.

"When the sky begins to darken, I envy my dead companions," said the young man, looking up at the sky as if searching for the faces of his remembered friends.

"It'll all be over soon. You'll go back home, see your family, be in your own home; you will fall in love and soon know that the nights can be as radiant as the days," she answered, brushing one of his arms with her fingertips.

Siegfried turned to her and timidly caressed the gold bracelet on her wrist.

"You are the sun...both at night and during the day..."

As he said this, his eyes slipped from his friend's naked tanned arms to the damp blond tips of her straight hair.

The girl looked at him and saw how her mother blushed. The afternoon filled with sadness. In rags, Manfred and Klaus also turned quite somber.

"It's better that we say goodbye right here..." said Barbara, stretching an arm out to them.

Manfred bent down and kissed her hand. One by one the others followed suit. The last man to kiss her was Siegfried who thoughtfully watched her leave. The two Barbaras had barely disappeared when the seven young men stared at one another and started back silently, each in his own world. They all imagined the same thing: the day when the world would let them take a girl by the hand and stroll through the countryside. They were all alone. While the vacationers dressed in white came and went, these prisoners were a small green stain: the announcement or memory of man's loneliness. They belonged to a world that no one wanted either to see or remember. They were a kind of rebuke.

"Germany is sealed off..." said Siegfried, one afternoon as the sun fell behind the hills.

Later Manfred had sung very softly "*Obs sturmt...*"

His voice rose through a special hole in the sky as if he weren't singing for this world, but for the memory of a fire that had fallen over them and which could not be transmitted. Siegfried's words and Manfred's song seemed terrible. Once back in town, the young girl remembered the words and the song and knew that outside of her, in some place, the world was not orange, blue, or pale rose as it was on the beach, but that there was something dark and terrifying lying in wait for her. She took hold of her mother's hand and they crossed the town square. At that time, it was crowded with people tanned by the sun. The small tables overflowed with talk and light outfits; filled with a light green liquid, the glasses sparkled. The two of them walked rapidly, trying not to look at the curious onlookers who greedily watched them go by. A moment later the prisoners skulked on the periphery, on their way to their cells. The vacationers eyed them with scorn, at times with hostility.

Barbara and her mother were in their room reading as they waited for dinner. Before going down to the dining room, they brushed their hair and changed from their shorts to light, low-necked, sleeveless outfits. The young men stared at them hungrily; they wanted to talk to the foreigners who were not interested in talking to them. Their disinterest provoked the contrary effect in the curious guests; after dinner they went in groups to dance until very late.

"What are the prisoners doing now?" asked Barbara, lifting her eyes toward her mother's.

Her mother stared back at her; in truth she had no idea what her young friends could be doing in prison. She remembered Siegfried's words: "The nights are even sadder than the days..." The nights were sad for her as well. Once the sun had set, she always found herself alone, facing a hollow, unresponsive world. She often imagined that eventually she would find happiness and never again have to face the voiceless shadows that awaited her every night. Her everyday doings, movements and words seemed absurd and empty to her. She felt she was moving around in a world that was mechanical and insensitive to her core and her need to be in touch with something warm and inviting. There were times she waited for her daughter to fall asleep so she could cry. In the dining room she realized that the tears of Siegfried and his friends must be even sadder because they were younger and it had to be even more difficult to understand things that she herself did not understand. What must the prison walls and talk be like? And why were they in jail? What had her friends done to deserve that final isolation? She walked across the dining room with a hostile expression: she was repulsed by the young men with sparkling hair who drank and talked loudly. "After all, they hadn't been in the fighting," she said to herself and chose to side with the prisoners.

She was reading when she heard a knock at her door. She opened it with curiosity. "We'd like you to come to the square with us...We'll be dancing the *farandole*."

It was one of those young men dressed in white who stared at her every night from a nearby table. He had hazel eyes and a sweet voice. Too bad he always wore an ascot around his neck; it made him resemble a movie gigolo. But all his friends dressed the same way.

"I can't leave my daughter by herself."

"Your daughter?" he asked, widening his eyes.

Barbara smiled smugly. The intruder now knew that his words and gestures would be fruitless. The girl, seated on her bed, glanced at the young man's white shirt and sullenly turned the pages of her book; then she looked at her mother who watched the young man with amusement. She remembered her friends, the prisoners, and a feeling of animosity flooded her chest. Why was her mother flirting with the intruder?

The young man introduced himself: "I'm Claude Defarge." He turned and left.

Barbara noticed how her mother sadly closed the door, as if she had closed it on the world. She dropped down slowly on the bed and thought for a while. Then she sat in front of the mirror and put on lipstick; her image sparkled in the mirror's quicksilver. She approached the balcony window and listened to the music rising from the square. It came in with the sounds of laughter, suffused with the ocean smell, riding upon a damp breeze.

"Come!" said Barbara, leaning her elbows on the window sill.

The girl jumped off her bed. Her mother took her in her arms and had her look down at the cobblestoned street which led to the square. Men and women were walking arm-in-arm, laughing, on their way to the party.

"Shall we go?" she asked.

Without waiting for a reply, she took the girl up in her arms, hummed a waltz, and danced around the room, sidestepping the furniture. Then she stopped, stood the young girl on her feet atop the bed, and dressed her in an English lace pinafore which left her shoulders and back bare. She put her in front of a mirror so she could see herself.

15

She brushed her hair and put her suntanned face next to her daughter's.

"Look, we're twins..."

Her English lace white dress also left her own arms and shoulders bare and she eerily resembled the young girl.

"Let's go," she said.

"But they aren't our friends..." the young girl said, frightened at the prospect of being alone with her mother in the company of strangers.

Barbara looked at her in supplication. "I'm just twenty-four..." she said, not realizing that her daughter couldn't understand what she wanted to say.

She fell back down on the edge of her bed, suddenly crestfallen.

"I used to think that the world was like it is tonight— full of music and lights...I didn't know that it was just a prison," she said sadly.

The word "prison" reminded the daughter of her German friends.

"Prison is for soldiers," she said, reminding her mother that she cared only for them.

"You know what, Barbara? I too am a beaten soldier..."

"You're unhappy?" the young girl asked.

They walked out holding hands. They walked down the street, following two young priests who were talking about a game of jai-alai. They walked behind them, trying to hear what they were saying. They were in serious discussion over the game. When they reached the square, mother and daughter sat down at a table away from the commotion. From there, they somberly watched the groups dancing happily. There was nothing to eat or drink but Pernod. Barbara ordered one for herself and her daughter watched her drink the greenish liquid. Groups of young men dressed in white pants eyed them. Barbara gestured to the waiter to come over.

"Where's the prison?" she asked calmly.

The waiter shot her a bewildered look, then lifted his eyes toward a gray stone building behind them, at a corner of the square. "It's there."

Mother and daughter looked at the building's small dark windows. The waiter left.

"That's where Karl, Manfred, Ernst, Klaus, Christian, Ric and Siegfried are," the girl said, looking at her mother who stared at the darkened windows. She saw her mother lower her eyes and slowly sip her Pernod; soon enough, her sadness fell over her daughter like a wall of dust and the party lost the sheen it had held a few minutes ago. For them, the party had receded so far that the two Barbaras could return to their world where defeat blew its gusts of tattered flags.

Suddenly Claude Defarge appeared, smiling; he leaned over their table, eyeing them with surprise.

"Care to dance?" he asked, showing his even teeth.

Barbara hesitated for a few seconds and then stood up.

"Wait for me. I'll be right back," she said to her daughter who, astonished, watched her slip into the crush of people.

The girl remained alone for a long time. Her mother had betrayed her and also her friends. She went back to the hotel alone. The entrance was lit up, but the corridors were dark. Unafraid, she opened the door to the room and looked through the suitcases for some chocolate bars. She went back down to the streets, cut through the circle of people dancing happily and headed for the prison. At the building entrance there were two whiskered men in uniform. The guards glanced curiously at her and then at each other. One of them bent down to talk to her.

"What do you want?"

"I want to see Siegfried," she answered rather firmly.

"The kraut?...I can't allow it! He's locked up," the man said, in an amused voice.

His companion looked her over, but she remained insistent.

"I want to see Siegfried," she repeated, raising her voice.

The guards started laughing. She sat down at the edge of a bench waiting for them to end their banter. The guards looked at her oddly. What was the little snotnose after? They quickly talked among themselves because the young girl's mute presence kept them from enjoying the party taking place just a few meters away.

After another few moments one of them approached the girl. "Well? What are you waiting for?"

"Siegfried," she answered firmly.

"I told you, he's locked up..."

The girl looked down at the cobblestones. Around the corner, in the square, people were still dancing. The music and the beat even reached the prison, snapping and rolling. The guards once again talked among themselves, this time more worriedly. The other guard now bent over Barbara.

"Are you going to wait all night?"

"Yes," said Barbara, hiding the chocolates among the folds of her white pinafore.

"Who are you? Where are you from?" the man asked, intrigued by her stubbornness.

"From Germany," she answered, knowing that these were important words to say.

The man ran back to his friend and Barbara saw that after a quick exchange of words, he vanished through the dark open door of the prison. Within seconds, the remaining guard approached her.

"Come here."

He took her by the hand and led her into the building.

They went through a door to a room with a rough wooden floor, two chairs and a couple of dusty wardrobes.

"He'll be right here."

Barbara waited in silence while the guard continued to watch her curiously. Within seconds, the other guard, followed by Siegfried, appeared. As soon as he saw her, standing there, with a serious look on her face, the young surprised prisoner could not speak. Barbara ran to hug his torn pants leg. The young man knelt down next to her and embraced her without saying a word. The guards left them alone.

"Mommy went dancing and I brought you chocolates," the young girl said, pulling out the bars and giving them to him.

Siegfried hugged her again without saying a word. He kissed the top of her head and kept his lips there for a long time. The girl put the chocolates in the pockets of his torn jacket.

"I don't love my mother..." she said, in confidence.

Siegfried pulled his face away from hers and looked into her very serious eyes.

"Hah!! Your mommy is right now looking for you in the crowd. We can see her from our cells," he said, reproaching her.

Barbara shrugged her shoulders.

"I don't care."

The young man placed his hands under her arms, lifted her up into the air and looked into her face for a few seconds; he then set her on his shoulders.

"Now you'll go to mommy. We'll all see each other tomorrow," he promised.

Siegfried called the guards and handed her to them. One stayed with the prisoner while the other accompanied the girl to the door. Once more Barbara was on the streets, surrounded by people she didn't know and who ignored her presence. She went back into the noisy square and looked for the table she had occupied with her mother. She was certain that Siegfried and his friends were watching her from a prison window and that unseen company made her feel less alone.

She saw her mother looking for her in the crowd; as she came closer, she saw Claude at her side. "Barbara! Where did you go?" her words rushed out.

Claude glared at her.

"To see Siegfried. He's very sad because you are dancing with him," she said, pointing to Claude, who now seemed angry.

Her mother glanced back toward the prison wall and said calmly: "Let's go to bed."

They went back to the hotel. The beat of the music even reached inside their room.

"I only love Siegfried," the young girl said, looking at her mother's bronze back.

"I do too," her mother said simply.

At the beach they could not pull themselves away from the company of Claude and his cousin Phillippe. They were always near, laughing and talking. They knew all the tourists; a chorus of young boisterous people formed around mother and daughter. They were driven to the neighboring villages, to drink *aperitifs* and see jai-alai games. On rainy days, they stayed in the club where the young men's aunts would invite them for tea. Claude and Phillippe knew everyone and their everyday, flashy life never seemed to end. Rarely did they talk about the recent war, and when they did, they spoke contemptuously, as if they wanted to mock their adversaries. War was a subject that held no interest for them.

If Barbara ever led the conversation back to the war,

when mention was made of the American landing, her friends would blush with anger. "Those damn savages!" they would say.

On the beach, above the cliffs, one could see the bunkers the Germans had built; behind the rock walls marking off the beach, the prisoners, their friends, were working. Sometimes, when Barbara dove into the ocean, she thought about them with remorse. To see them now, they would sneak out during the afternoon siesta, when the tide covered the sand and the waves smashed against the rocks. They would rush out and make their way to where the prisoners split rocks. The young men would sense their arrival and stop working to watch them approach. And when they sat down on the rocks, the young men would gather around them and talk a little. They knew that their friends were no longer alone. Barbara felt a bit guilty. She wished she could do something for them, but she couldn't even say a word in their favor. She would gaze upon their bodies burnt by sun and wind, and a kind of shame crept over her. She hardly tried to look at Siegfried who watched her from the depths of his blue eyes.

"We came running..." the young girl said one day.

The young prisoners barely smiled, their green uniforms turning grayer by the day. Their blond hair was covered with the chalky rock dust, and they resembled men sentenced to vanish in the dry ground.

"We had to escape from Claude," the girl added.

Barbara threw her cigarette away angrily. "Someone has to do something. You can't go on like this..."

She looked at Siegfried leaning against his pickax and then at the others; their lips were cracked and split from the dust, and they seemed forever exhausted. No one ever spoke anymore about studies or families. Siegfried placed his chin on the handle of his pickax as if he were thinking.

Barbara glanced at her daughter and then at herself: they both looked as if they had just walked out of a cool, starched place; the sheen of their sea-roughened skin stood out against the white cloth of their shorts. A huge distance separated them from the beaten and ragged young men, and she did not know how to bridge the gap. She no longer brought them gifts; she did not want to draw attention to their different worlds. Now the young girl was the one who brought the cigarettes and sweets, which they humbly accepted. She knew that when they returned to town, the soldiers would stay splitting rocks, more alone and ever more hopeless than before their friendship.

Karl was sitting next to her; Barbara lifted her hand and ran it through his hair. The young man let himself be caressed, and his companions looked down and said nothing. The memories of their war experiences reached her through the four o'clock sun, and she looked upon them, stupefied: they had survived something terrible. Many men had been driven crazy by the thousands of airplanes strafing them. Now they were facing her, like inhabitants of another planet: with clear eyes, they looked out at the silent world, motionless in their abandonment.

The young girl also felt the afternoon's profound eeriness and stayed quietly at Siegfried's side. She didn't want to go back either to the hotel or the party to which they had been invited. Her mother felt the same way.

"They never let you go to the beach?" Barbara asked, trying to sound casual.

Manfred started laughing, then stifled his laughter. The others merely shook their heads. Siegfried stopped building the house of stone he had been constructing for the young girl and looked up in surprise. Then he went back to his game. He, the mother, and the young girl would live in the house. Barbara transformed her fingers into legs that could walk, he did the same, and they both went inside the little house which was situated in a far-off country where hatred did not exist.

"Come and live with us!" the young girl screamed to her mother.

They all gathered around the house and asked for asylum. Siegfried's, Barbara's and her mother's hands came and went inside the house through the door-like holes and they invited in friends. When the game ended and the sun was going down, they all walked together toward town. They walked in groups: Siegfried at her mother's side, not speaking. Manfred on the other side of the path. The girl with Karl and Ric following behind, and close by, Ernst, Christian and Klaus. They all stared at the orange sun that at the moment dropped over the green fields and created lakes and mirrors. High above, the cloudless sky turned from one shade of blue to another, with the pine trees reflected in its smooth surface.

> *Wie mein Glück ist mein Leid*
> *Willst du im Abendrot*
> *Froh dich baden? Hindweg ist's,*
> *Und die Erde ist kalt,*
> *Und der Vogel der Nacht schwirrt*
> *Unbequem vor das Auge dir.*

The Hölderlin stanza, recited in Siegfried's deep voice, rose above the reddened hills that at the moment began to grow pale; the cold ocean breeze blew over them and the group of young people said nothing. They would share the afternoon's beauty and the approaching night's melancholy.

Barbara turned to Siegfried. "Thanks for sharing this afternoon with me," she said, certain that he could accept the afternoon's beauty without bitterness.

"It's harder to bear beauty than sorrow when you are alone," he answered, stopping in front of her and gazing right into her eyes.

His friends had stopped at a turn in the path a few meters back. Barbara felt the solitude of the impending darkness all around them and could only see the sparkle in the young man's eyes coming dangerously close to hers. She felt his hands on her naked shoulders and the touch of his lips upon hers. A car passed near them and slowed down, almost stopped.

"Nazi pigs!" shouted a woman leaning out the window. And to make her words more real, she spat on Barbara.

The car suddenly pulled off and Barbara stood wiping the spit off her face. Siegfried blushed, was about to say something, when his friends appeared with the girl's hand in theirs.

When they saw Barbara they knew what had happened.

"You shouldn't be seen with us," said Klaus. He approached her, looked at her, unable to do a thing.

"What's wrong, mommy?" asked the young girl, running up to her mother.

"Nothing...They just spat on me," Barbara said coldly, unable to hold back the tears running down her cheeks.

"Go on ahead," said Siegfried. He gestured for his friends to take the girl away so she wouldn't see her mother weeping.

The young men started walking, clutching the girl's hand; she let them lead her without looking back. She knew that something awful had happened, though she had no clear idea who or why someone had spat in her mother's face. They walked on like this for a while. Suddenly she glanced back and saw the outline of Siegfried and her mother as they shone brilliantly against the darkness, as if a halo circled around their blond hair and their golden bodies tanned by the sun. They were very far behind. Ahead of the girl and her friends the first roofs of the town appeared.

"Barbara, you are my first love..." said Siegfried, with eyes cast down, as his friends walked far ahead.

"And you are the first person to love me," Barbara answered, almost ashamed, as she stood in front of that young man who looked upon her with such intensity.

The young man removed a blade of grass which had gotten stuck to her hair; he placed it in the palm of his open hand and blew softly.

"This is how much I mean to you," he said unhappily.

"You?... No, you are not the tiny leaf that stayed on Siegfried's shoulder," she said trying to lighten the conversation that was growing dangerous.

He held in his questioning silence.

"You are Siegfried, the warrior," she said, at that moment very sure of her words.

Later, in the hotel, she could not sleep. It was foolish to let that young boy fall in love with her. And yet she had not led him on; it had happened on its own, in spite of her. She remembered his clear eyes and felt like crying. The woman's spitting had had a strange effect on her; the stupid hatred, the rejection of the woman who confused her own ugliness with things unrelated to her, made Barbara feel a part of Siegfried. The woman's hatred had placed them all together, merged her with those young men in a very mysterious way. She could never again separate herself from them. The insult had made Barbara one of them. She fell asleep feeling that something mysterious joined her to Siegfried and his friends.

Her daughter also realized that something important had just sealed their friendship with the Germans. She lay down quietly next to her mother and thought about how Siegfried had looked at her. She wanted to know what it was that the young man saw in her and happily recalled that he had told her that she resembled her mother in the way one drop of water resembles another.

The following day, on the beach, Barbara anxiously awaited the noon meal so that they could rejoin the prisoners. Claude and Phillippe happily sat around her, but she hardly heard their conversation. Claude tried to scold her: the night before she had stood them up. He had waited for her until quite late to go to Silvie's party. Barbara heard them without really understanding. She was thinking about Siegfried and his friends who at that moment would be doing what they always did: splitting rocks in order to open a shorter path to the beach they never visited. Her daughter, right next to her, was building a sand house which resembled the one built the evening before with Siegfried.

"What a pretty house!" said Claude, trying to act amiably to the child who eyed him with so much scorn.

"The house is for Siegfried, my mother and me," she said seriously.

"Siegfried?" Claude asked.

"We already have two homes: one in the country, the other on the beach," she said looking sarcastically at him.

When they got back to town, Claude and Phillippe insisted they get into the car. The two Barbaras suspected something was up because instead of taking the normal route back to the hotel, they took a detour and soon were driving to the spot where the Germans worked. Claude drove slowly, as if he were looking for something or knew the area. When Barbara realized the route they were taking, she looked distrustfully at her friend and blushed. The girl sat alertly in her seat. Soon they were in front of the prisoners. The girl called them each by name and they straightened up surprised. Barbara leaned over, stuck her hand out the window to wave goodbye to them.

The Germans remained standing, watching them pass.

"I don't know how you can wave to those animals," Claude rebuked her angrily.

"Those soldiers are friends of mine," she said quite seriously.

"Friends? Are you a Nazi, Barbara?" Claude asked unpleasantly.

"A Nazi?" Barbara started laughing.

Claude was furious. Phillippe looked at her, annoyed. An embarrassing silence followed. All three were angry: she well understood that they had intentionally driven by the Germans and that provocation made her angry; for their part, they thought that it was unbecoming for a lady to talk to those filthy bums.

"There were Nazis when Hitler was winning...lots of them. Now it's just a question of young defeated soldiers. 'Offer a silver bridge to the fleeing enemy,'" Barbara said in reproach. She glanced sarcastically at the well-dressed young men who were with her in the car.

By the time they reached the hotel, the friendship had cooled considerably. They avoided exchanging glances in the dining room. Phillippe apparently had invited another woman for coffee and Claude joined them on the terrace. From there he shot secret glances back at the foreigner; she, lost in her own thoughts, had forgotten he existed.

Barbara was sure Phillippe had told all the guests about her friendship with the Germans. People who hours earlier had smiled in a friendly manner now glared at them from the neighboring tables. She felt unbearably alone and foreign among those well-tailored women and those men who wore ascots around their throats and spoke enthusiastically about the huge selection in the black market, while savoring South American coffee. She went up to her room, almost on the verge of tears. She cared nothing for the silence of people. She would never relinquish Siegfried, to whom she owed her love, nor the others, to whom she owed her friendship.

"Are you sad, mommy?" asked Barbara, looking at her mother.

"Me, sad?...I am angry," she replied, lifting her head and looking at the tall pines that rose above the back of the church tower.

Just then someone knocked on the door.

"Come in!" Barbara said sharply.

Miss Gabrielle tiptoed in and stood looking at her without knowing what to say. Barbara watched her embarrassed posture, her hands red from working too hard and her absurdly short hair which made her look ridiculous.

"Look here!" she said, touching the ends of her hair with one hand.

Barbara watched openmouthed, not sure what the woman wanted to say to her.

"Look! It's growing back now...They killed him...Don't see them again," she said almost in a whisper.

Barbara understood: Miss Gabrielle had collaborated with the Germans and after liberation, they had shaven her head as a punishment.

"You collaborated?" Barbara asked, also in a whisper.

"No. I lived with a German...I was in love with him and they killed him," she said in the no-nonsense voice of a woman who seemed incapable of loving anyone or being loved by anyone.

"You lived with him?"

"Yes, but I was not a collaborator. They're the collaborators," she said, pointing downstairs with her index finger.

"Those downstairs?"

"Yes. Mr. Defarge, Mr. Duclos, Mr. De France, that's why

28

they're so afraid...and millions of others," she said with a sigh.

Barbara offered her a cigarette to calm her down, since she seemed seized by panic.

"Don't worry about me, I'm a foreigner," she said softly.

"You never know...It's better if you don't see them again," said the woman, recalling something that still terrified her.

Barbara said nothing. Her daughter stared at Miss Gabrielle with almost gaping eyes.

"We can't see Siegfried again?" she asked.

"No, young lady, you can't. Something could happen to them..." she answered, still looking frightened.

"It all happened barely a few days ago. Barely a few days ago he was here...then they took him away...they started killing him on the way there...they dragged him through the square."

The girl and her mother listened in silence and then watched her withdraw from their hotel room, touching her cropped hair. She closed the door and walked down the hallway. The two Barbaras felt oppressed by the woman's revelation. They, in fact, didn't know what to do; they went toward the balcony, rested their elbows on the windowsill, and for a while looked out upon the sky and the church tower. No matter what, they should go and see them, especially since they had driven by them in Claude's car, and yet...Miss Gabrielle's serious face paralyzed them. The mother picked up a book, stretched out on the bed to read, but couldn't understand what she was reading. The words seemed so hollow; she kept thinking about Siegfried and his friends who at that moment were splitting rocks. It was strange; when she wanted to think about nothing, when she felt disoriented as she did now, it never occurred to her to think about her house or her husband. Her husband seemed to her to be the strangest person in her life, the one responsible for making her strange to the rest of the world. His disregard had thrown her into a kind of solitude where she could hold on to nothing. She wanted to run out and throw her arms around the neck of the young man responsible for her being spat upon the evening before. Instead, she slammed her book shut and sunk her head into the pillows.

"Barbara, let's take a nap!"

The young girl lay down on her bed and saw how quickly her mother fell asleep. As soon as she was sure her mother was sleeping, she left the room, raced down the stairs, crossed the hotel lobby under the uncaring eyes of the other guests and made for the path that led to where her friends were. She arrived running. From far off she had seen them bending down as they worked; their green uniforms on the yellow rock charged her with emotion. She stood among them and all but Siegfried smiled; he only gazed upon her in fear, as if asking: "Why didn't she come?"

The young girl rushed to answer the question posed by Siegfried's expression. "She's sleeping."

Siegfried sat on a rock and toyed with the smaller stones, absorbed in thought, allowing the girl and his companions to look at him. Barbara stared at his suntanned hands; anything to do with him intrigued her deeply, his simplest gestures were mysterious and held meaning. Through him she had discovered the unknown mystery in surfaces, lights and words. Siegfried was as unknowable as the characters in the Viking tales that her mother had given her. She couldn't understand why he was a prisoner instead of sailing away between the rocks and the sea. She would certainly get in the boat with him and sail back to Viking lands.

"Siegfried."

The young man lifted his eyes. Manfred was gesturing for him to respond to the young girl who was looking at him in such pain.

"Come here!"

Barbara walked over and Siegfried sat her next to him. The other prisoners stopped working and gathered about them.

"Miss Gabrielle told mommy how they killed her German friend and she fell asleep," Barbara said, by way of explanation.

They played for a while and then went back to work. Barbara helped to carry the small rocks they gave her. And there, in the countryside, open for all to see, without objects to fight over, without interests, with no past or future, the slightest gestures were full of meaning. Barbara would never forget their voices or their actions. While they split the rocks, they would make-believe they were precious stones and then baptize them with names before giving them to her.

"This emerald is for Barbara," and they would give her a pebble she would store at the side of the path.

Each stone had a secret history. Sometimes Siegfried, at other times Klaus or Christian, would relate the legend.

"Did you tell your mother that you were coming to see us?" Ric suddenly asked her.

"Yes...I did..." Barbara lied.

"Will she come to pick you up?" Siegfried asked hopefully.

"Yes...if Miss Gabrielle lets her..."

"Who is Miss Gabrielle?" Christian asked.

"The one whose German friend was killed..." Barbara said, in a whisper.

The young men looked at each other and said nothing.

"She told my mother that they dragged him through the

square..." said Barbara, looking all around her, as if in fear.

"Miss Gabrielle is very afraid," she said, listening to the late afternoon that wheeled silently over their heads.

She looked at each one of them. "I'm not afraid," she said, through the silence of her friends.

"If your mother doesn't come, we'll take you back," said Siegfried, also watching how the late afternoon hummed about them.

They took her far from the path and almost hid her behind a few rocks they were breaking. They then brought her the stones which they had recently baptized with new names. She had to hide both herself and the treasures so that the evil men wouldn't come and steal them. But Barbara knew that they weren't hiding her for her treasures alone, and yet she decided to play along. From within her hiding place, she gazed upon them, smiling, happy to share a secret with them. From there, she saw them checking the sky for the sun as it moved slowly across the sky, never taking her eyes off the blond heads of the Germans. A dry heat rose from the rocks and drank the moisture that came from the unseen beach. From time to time, Siegfried glanced at the abandoned path. "He's waiting for her," the girl said to herself, as she realized how often her friend would look at the spot from which her mother would appear. She thought that he loved her, more than she loved him, and she felt very sad. She called out to him, and the young man politely came over.

"Siegfried, I love you a lot."

The young man tousled her hair as if playing with a cat and then went off to find a precious stone.

"This one's my heart," he said in all seriousness.

The young girl put the stone in the pocket of her shorts. When she returned to her home, she would hide it in a tiny red velvet bag that her mother had sewn for her for when she played Mommy. There she also stored the plastic leg of a doll who had drowned in the bathtub and a dry beetle she had found in Lamartine Square.

All of a sudden Barbara heard her mother running toward them. Her sandals were slapping the path. The girl raised her head and she saw Siegfried running to meet her mother. She saw them speaking with each other for a few seconds and then the young man put an arm around her shoulders and she hid her head in his ripped jacket as if about to cry. They stayed like that for a few minutes. Then her mother seemed to get hold of herself and she and Siegfried walked over to where the others were working, smiling, as they awaited them.

"She's there, hiding behind the rocks. She's very wealthy. That's why she's hiding," Klaus said.

Barbara came over to her daughter and stared at her. "You really frightened me," she said.

"You fell asleep so I came..." said Barbara, glad to see that her mother had been frightened by her absence.

She sat next to her daughter, hidden behind the rocks, and stayed there like that for a while, worried. Siegfried, on the other hand, seemed to be beaming. He sat facing her without saying a word.

Barbara took the stone out of her shorts and showed it to her mother. "Look, this is Siegfried's heart. He gave it to me," she said proudly.

The young man lowered his eyes and then caressed Barbara's toes sticking out through the straps of her sandals. The mother picked up another pebble and gave it to him.

"And this is mine," she said to him.

He stared at the pebble and then put it in the pocket closest to his heart.

Then mother and daughter decided to go back to town. Miss Gabrielle's words had frightened Barbara. Siegfried accompanied them back to the path to say goodbye. He bowed reverentially and kissed the young woman's hand. Confused, she embraced his shoulders and gave him a quick kiss on his sun-dried, dusty lips.

"Siegfried, you are made from the tiny membrane covering the linden leaf," she said looking into the young man's blue eyes sparkling fully in the afternoon light.

"What you've said is quite beautiful," he said, accepting his vulnerability.

He followed them with his eyes until they disappeared. Then he returned to his friends waiting for him.

At night, while Barbara and her mother were getting ready for bed, someone knocked on the door. It was Claude. He seemed unkempt, and he looked at Barbara with glowing eyes. From her bed, the little girl could see the dark brilliance in the young man's eyes.

"I need to speak to you," he begged.

Barbara gestured that the young girl would hear him. Claude took her hand and led her into the hallway.

"I'll be back in an hour," he said angrily.

The young woman watched him go down the corridor, sure and determined, without once glancing back. She went back in the room and closed the door thoughtfully. She felt her daughter scornfully eyeing her. She took off her dress and got into bed.

"Let's go to sleep," she said, turning the light off immediately.

But she could not sleep, she was sure that Claude would come back and knock on the door. She did not like her friend's daring ways. She had made a mistake that other night when she went to dance the *farandole*. Yet, she consoled herself, sooner or later she would have to talk to him. She was upset that he would be returning so late. She would have to go out of her room not to have to argue at the door. What kind of conversation would it be? She wasn't sure, but she knew there would be one. She half-opened her eyes and saw her daughter watching her through the darkness. She preferred not to talk to her and feigned sleep. After a while she heard the even breathing of her daughter, who had fallen asleep. Very cautiously she slipped out of bed, got dressed and waited. Soon someone knocked softly on the door; she opened the door and stepped out quickly, closing it very carefully.

"I've never done this before," she reproached Claude.

"Let's go," he ordered.

"Where? I can't leave my daughter alone."

"Wait here."

Claude ran down the hall and returned seconds later with Miss Gabrielle.

"You'll watch the girl until we get back, right?"

Miss Gabrielle nodded without questioning. She tiptoed into the room and carefully closed the door.

Claude took Barbara by the hand and dragged her to the car.

"Where are we going?" Barbara asked, frightened.

"To my cousin Silvie's house."

They drove through the sea-drenched night. The salty wind stuck to their hair and made their skin damp. Claude parked the car by some huge boulders and got out. Barbara followed him. She knew that Silvie's house was somewhere between the hill and the rocks. They took a pebbly path that smelled of oregano and salt, and soon were on a kind of terrace formed by rocks. From there you could see the sparkling ocean below. Above them, was the deep and endless sky. The beauty of the place made Barbara remember Siegfried; she would have liked to share this beauty with him. "It is more difficult to bear beauty than sorrow when you're alone," he had told her one evening. And

Barbara felt that she could not bear the beauty of that night suspended halfway between the sky and the ocean.

Claude approached her from behind and tried to kiss her.

"No, Claude!" she said brusquely.

The young man glared at her. "You tease! You've been leading me on."

"Me?" she was about to laugh, but she held back when she saw the fury in his eyes.

"Yes...you..."

He grabbed her shoulders, kissed her on the lips as she struggled away from him. His behavior seemed ridiculous and offensive.

When she was able to pull herself away from him, she said: "Take me back to the hotel."

Claude seemed about to collapse. "I'm sorry, Barbara, but I don't understand you...Did I offend you?...What can I do to make things right?"

Barbara held her tongue and began going down the pebbly path they had taken to get there. She almost tripped in the darkness without having Claude's hand to guide her. He rushed to help her.

"Let's go to Silvie's house for a while...there you'll forget what I did," he begged.

Barbara relented. It was such a gorgeous night that she felt it was unfair to go back and lock herself up in her room. Also, once things had started, she wanted to find out how far they'd go. They wandered a bit until they were at the door of Silvie's half-hidden house. Elegantly dressed people she knew were in the foyer and on the terrace, either drinking or dancing in small groups. Silvie came out to welcome them. Soon they were dancing among couples who barely moved they were so busy kissing. Phillippe was there, silently watching what was going on around him. He seemed obsessed with Silvie, who went past without seeing him.

"Does he like Silvie?" Barbara asked.

Claude started laughing.

"We're all three cousins. Silvie is engaged to Bertrand," he said, pointing him out. Bertrand was talking to a much older man.

At that moment Silvie passed by and looked at her, almost scornfully, as if she had just been speaking about her or as if she felt annoyed by the foreigner's low neckline and loose hair. All the other women had short dresses, pleated with beeswax, but with the back and shoulders covered. And their hair was up in a chignon. Moreover, they weren't wearing sandals, but shoes with soles three to four centimeters thick.

Barbara realized she was dressed and coiffured differently and this made her suspicious to those bourgeoisie women who ate, drank and danced in moderation. Maybe that's why Claude had acted so outrageously minutes earlier.

"Why doesn't Phillippe come and say hello to me?" she asked.

Claude bit his lips, then looked straight at her. "Because of what happened with the Germans. You don't understand it, you're a foreigner, but for us, the occupation is something we can't forget," he said proudly.

"But that has nothing to do with it. The war's over and prisoners shouldn't be treated like common criminals," Barbara said.

Claude stared at her in amazement. He drew closer and whispered: "I hope you're not in a fix with one of those guys."

Barbara wanted to return to her hotel at once, but this was not an option. She was too far away and, besides, she didn't want to quarrel with Claude who was the only one still treating her nicely.

"Yes, Claude, I'm in love with one of them," she said defiantly.

Claude didn't take her seriously. He started laughing and took her out to dance.

"You're so sentimental," he said, sure of his words.

It was odd for Silvie not to dance with Bertrand, and it was even stranger that Phillippe didn't invite her to dance either and just followed her around with his eyes. When Claude drove Barbara back to the hotel, Phillippe came with them. He seemed to have forgiven Barbara for her friendship with the prisoners, since he made no mention of it.

"Phillippe, don't let Silvie marry Bertrand," Barbara insisted.

"Me? I'm not crazy," Phillippe answered.

Claude laughed. Barbara had no idea what was going on. The two men seemed to share a secret.

Later that night, almost at daybreak, someone knocked on her door. Barbara sat up in bed and listened, terrified at the relentless knocking. She preferred not to answer: she was sure it was Claude. Outside the wind blew over the hills and banged the blinds on the balcony. She listened to the night, which now seemed to howl. She felt alone and abandoned. Why was Claude knocking at her door at this time of the night? It embarrassed her; she angrily chewed her lips. Maybe it would be better if she returned to Paris; her vacation was becoming much too complicated. But the thought of returning home paralyzed her. Return to what? To the loneliness of her rooms? To her lunches and dinners all by herself? Attended by Teodoro who watched her, shaking his head in pity? She remembered her bedroom, her splendid fireplace, and herself always alone in the middle

of that awful winter cold without coal or affection. She
buried her head in her pillows.

"Barbara!...Barbara!..." It wasn't Claude's voice, but that
of a woman.

She got out of bed and slowly opened the door. Silvie
stood before her, agitated.

"What's wrong?"

The young woman came in with a scrunched-up face
and fell right into her bed.

Barbara came over to her and shook her by the shoulders. It was useless.

Silvie didn't want to talk. Barbara stood waiting for
quite a while. She had no idea what had happened. She
glanced at her daughter who, sitting up in bed, seemed to
be watching Silvie with amazement.

"What's going on? Why aren't you at home?" Barbara
asked, but she did not receive an answer.

Silvie's frozen expression frightened her. Her daughter
began to cry in her bed; she too was scared by the mute,
pale woman lying on her mother's bed. Barbara tried to turn
her over and when she did, she noticed that the young
woman was completely naked under her raincoat. Scared,
she dropped her back on the bed.

"I'm going to go find her cousins!" she said to her
daughter, who was still crying.

She rushed out into the hall, trying to remember
Claude's room number. She couldn't, so she went down to
the front desk and called him from there. Claude didn't
seem at all perturbed.

"Silvie?...Just ignore her."

Barbara understood neither Claude's indifference nor
Silvie's behavior. She returned to her room, puzzled. She
looked strangely at the young woman, who remained flat
and motionless. Barbara felt odd around her and her

cousins. She did not understand them. She decided to lie down in her daughter's bed and wait for daybreak.

Now with the sunlight streaming in, the events of the night seemed even stranger. When Barbara awoke, Silvie was gone. She worried while she ate breakfast. Her daughter looked at her without understanding anything either, and she didn't know what kind of explanation to give. They went to the beach, feeling lonelier than before. The only ones who seemed familiar and whom she understood were her German friends. She thought of them gratefully and remembered Siegfried's dusty face tenderly. She stretched out on the beach hoping not to run into the others.

A familiar voice greeted her. "What did that crazy Silvie do?"

It was Claude. He sprawled next to her and began to play with her loose hair. Barbara moved away to see him better.

"Nothing. She came into my room and lay down on the bed without saying a word. I thought she was ill."

Amused, Claude looked at her. Then he leaned over her and whispered in confidence: "She went into Phillippe's room, stark naked. When he wanted to make love to her, she came into my room without telling me that she had gone to Phillippe's room for several nights running. She also behaved queerly with me. When I threw her out, she went to your room. She wanted to start trouble."

Barbara looked at him incredulously. "Why? Why would she do that?"

Claude shrugged his shoulders and laughed. "She likes to tease men. It amuses her," he said calmly.

Barbara felt very uneasy. She could not believe that the young man lying next to her could calmly accept a creature as strange as Silvie. Claude, on the other hand, did not understand why Barbara criticized his behavior. Silvie then appeared, pale and mysterious, and stretched out next to them. Later Phillippe arrived. Nothing different from the day before. They all seemed to have forgotten the incident that had so terrified her the previous night. Barbara looked at them in amazement. She wanted to leave.

She went off to swim with her daughter, but couldn't avoid returning to town with them.

In the hotel dining room, she observed from her table that the cousins looked at her as before. They seemed to be two strangers she had never seen and yet found everywhere: on trains, in restaurants, in theaters. They were part of that huge crowd of young people seeking superficial adventures, who surround lonely women as if they were simple, short-term treasures.

She got up and locked herself in her room. The world was an unpleasant place. It was peopled by greedy strangers who lay in wait for her everywhere. She did not dare go looking for her German friends. She was afraid that her intimacy with them could cause them some kind of trouble. Besides, she was worried about Siegfried. She knew that the young man's love was dangerous and heartrending. Nothing positive for either of them could come of it. On the contrary, it could bring him harm. She couldn't admit that it could harm her as well: a kind of inner censor wouldn't allow her this thought. What could she do? Stay locked in her room to escape the dangerous company of strangers and the affection of her friends, this double-edged sword? She yearned to have someone, someone to tell that she was confused, and wanted to see, more than anything else, a young soldier in rags waiting for her near some rocks. But to whom could she confess something so serious? To no one. She tried to read, then decided to get a sheet of paper; she sat at her desk. She didn't know to whom to write. She was confused facing the blank paper. Maybe she would write to

Siegfried. No. She decided to write her husband one of those impersonal and polite letters they were used to exchanging. She dated the letter.

"Mommy? Aren't we going to the beach?" asked her daughter, who was playing next to her.

"No, I'm going to write a few letters."

The young girl said nothing. She knew her mother was preoccupied and that they would spend the afternoon locked in the room. She sank her head into the pillow to read. Then she raised her eyes and saw her mother hunched over the table. No, they would not be going out but she did not want to stay. She wanted to go to the beach. She was also upset by the events of the night before. The memory of Silvie's body on her mother's bed still remained, invading all corners of the room, absorbing the oxygen.

"Mommy, aren't we going to the beach?"

Her mother grew testy. "Let me write."

She stepped over to the balcony and inhaled the afternoon's seabreeze. The room, in contrast, was hot and smelled of Silvie.

"I want to go to the beach."

Her mother was angry. She went back to her letter and tore it up. It wasn't the letter she needed to write. The only person she really wanted to write to was Siegfried. She crossed her arms on the desk and buried her head. She remained like that for quite a while. Then she decided to write him a letter. Maybe she wouldn't give it to him, but she wanted to say that she didn't want to see him again because, in fact, she just wanted to see him all the time. Then she would return to Paris. She weighed each word. But each was either too blunt or too evasive. Once more she put her head down on her arms. Still, she could not leave without saying goodbye. And she could not stay: her intimacy with Silvie and Claude had made the hotel suffocating. After Claude had made unwanted advances to her the previous night, she did not know how to handle him. He was very different from her and she did not know how to explain that to him. Maybe it was a weakness of hers, but she felt trapped. She realized that this would be the time the Germans would be waiting for her arrival, and still she remained where she was, motionless, without daring to go, daring to stay, daring to write. She dozed off for a while, her head on her crossed arms. The silence of her room awakened her. She turned to look for her daughter, but she was not in the room. She went into the hall and called out. Barbara did not answer. Frightened, she went down to the reception desk.

"Have you seen Barbara?" she asked, scared.

"Yes...she went out more than two hours ago. She was carrying a sand pail," slurred an employee, his voice full of wine.

Barbara ran out. Surely her daughter had gone off to join her friends. She ran down the path that led to where the prisoners were. The path seemed longer than it had the evening before. She didn't know why, but she was almost certain that this time her daughter had not gone looking for them. The four o'clock afternoon sun lit up the trees and hills and struck her forehead and eyes. She saw the prisoners from far away, bending over the earth as if they were part of it. There was harmony between nature and their pure, agile bodies. They heard her approaching; Christian and Siegfried went out to meet her. They stopped short.

"She's not here?" she asked, out of breath.

"No...she hasn't come..." they said to her, frightened.

She felt the ground opening under her feet. She looked hopelessly at Siegfried.

"I wasn't paying attention...I was writing you a letter and she went out..."

Siegfried tried to calm her. "She must be playing in town."

The others gathered around her and exchanged words. Within seconds they had planned a search. They would divide up: some would go to town, others into the hills, and she and Siegfried would look for her at the hotel and the beach. The beach! At this time of day there would be no beach. The tide overran the sand and reached up to the cliffs. They would all meet back by the cliffs where the beach would be covered by the tide. She, Siegfried and Ric ran to town. Above all, she should inquire at the hotel. The others waited for her near the prison. They did not want to be seen for fear that they would be held, and could not help her. The clerk at the hotel saw her return sweating and all red from running.

"I'm telling you that she left here more than two hours ago," he repeated, bored.

"Who? The girl? We saw her going off toward the beach path. She had her sand pail with her," said a woman who coolly stretched out her hand to pick up her room key.

Barbara saw Claude and Phillippe having a drink on the terrace. She approached them.

"The girl? No, we didn't see her. But she must be around here somewhere. She's very willful—" said Claude, quite naturally.

Barbara went back to the square, seeking assurance from Siegfried and Ric, who waited for her at a corner, hidden from sight.

"It seems she went to the beach," she said flatly.

Without delay, they searched around a few houses and then took a shortcut to the beach. From high on the cliffs, they could see that it was under water. The rough surf reached the stone wall and angrily crashed against it. From high up Barbara sought out her daughter's white bathing suit and blond hair, and saw nothing but the furious volley of waves. Her friends looked at her with concern. They also scanned the waves and the rocks without success, then walked up and down the cliffs hopelessly looking for tracks of Barbara. Far off, beyond the cliffs, they saw the other Germans, also fruitlessly searching for her. They signaled back and forth to each other.

"The current's too strong," said Christian gloomily, gazing out at the blue sea turning to white foam at his feet. Barbara sat down on the rocks and held her blowing hair in her hands. She was confused, unable to move. How could this happen to her? She gazed hopelessly at the immensity spread out below her feet. Siegfried crouched next to her.

"Barbara is safe somewhere. I know it," he said authoritatively.

He gave her his hand and lifted her up to continue looking. They searched about the craggy boulders without success. Suddenly they heard a voice calling them from afar. The voice carried by the wind was resonant and with a hint of victory. Manfred was calling, pointing to a spot they could not distinguish. They went toward it, stumbling and regaining their balance so as not to fall twenty or thirty meters down. With his uniform blowing in the wind, Manfred waited for them smiling. He pointed to a spot twenty meters below. There, on a tiny ledge formed by the wall of rocks, was Barbara's diminutive body sunning itself. Her white shorts and her hair sparkled in the sun. Barbara sat down to watch her daughter. The others did the same. The waves stopped a few centimeters from the girl and then roared in retreat. Soon they would march up and carry her off. How could they reach her first? They had to go back to where the beach had been and from there swim along the edge of the rocks to reach her. Or else go down the sheer cliff to get to her. Barbara decided on the former. She was a good swimmer. Siegfried would go with her. The others, meanwhile, would watch from above.

"It's better to climb down. The currents are too strong. Many of our men drowned here," said Christian, getting ready to scale the wall.

Barbara raced across the cliffs toward the beach. Siegfried and Ric went with her while Manfred and Christian got ready to climb down the cliff. Ric wouldn't let her dive into the water. Siegfried was signaling for him to hold her back.

"We'll wait here. Siegfried is a good swimmer," he said calmly.

She looked at Siegfried whose sparkling teeth shone through his smile. He seemed grateful to be able to do something for her. It all happened so fast: she saw him take off his jacket and boots, all the while watching her with his twinkling eyes. Then she saw him approach, bend down; she felt his lips divided by the dust on her cheek and his wide hand on her hair. She watched him hurl himself into the waves. Squatting next to her, Ric lit one of the cigarettes her daughter had offered them each day and smoked it, staring stubbornly at the ground. His hand rested reassuringly on her bare shoulders. A stronger will than hers obliged her to remain still. Siegfried swam deeper into the sea looking for the route that would take him to where the young girl was.

"I'll return with her in just a few minutes," he had said before plunging into the water.

Several difficult minutes passed. Neither of the two said a word. Christian threw his cigarette away; half-closing his pale eyelids, he examined the sea. He turned around to look at her; he had a serious expression and his eyes revealed anxiety. Barbara understood that he feared for two people: for the young girl and for his friend.

The young man lowered his head. "Siegfried loves you," he said softly.

"And I love him," she replied simply.

And they waited a moment that grew and expanded the way a voice does in a microphone. The woman stared out at the useless afternoon and also at her useless body. Nothing had meaning. She glanced at Christian's knee, covered by the green serge of his uniform, so close to hers and then at him looking out over the water and the light. What did it all mean? Why did absurd things, like her daughter's silly escapade and the pointless imprisonment of those young men, have to happen? And what about herself: what was she doing there but waiting for the unexpected end to that absurd situation? It all happened in the blink of an eye: her daughter's entrance into the world. She tried to remember what her life had been like without her but couldn't. Barbara had always been at her side. It was silly to think that she had not been with her at one time. She had also known those young men as well. They had been in her life for all her years. She had the feeling that they had always been with her and that she would always be near their green uniforms. Also everything—her daughter, her friends, she herself—would vanish in a blink of an eye, as suddenly as they had first appeared in this world. They lived within a dazzling and fleeting minute that heartwrenchingly united them—they were all one, and she and her daughter Barbara were part of that everything. The rest was unreal, and that is why her daughter had fled the fantastic and unwanted presence of Silvie and Claude. She did not belong to that foreign time of those unknown friends in the hotel. A hodgepodge of stale words fell on her head and darkened her vision.

"The girl? ...she went to the beach..." Their voices didn't heed boundaries, and that's why they were not anywhere near her and why they didn't form part of who she was. "I'll return with her in just a few minutes." It was Siegfried's voice bringing her back to the reality of that minute that would never end.

She glanced at Christian's cigarette butt, now falling apart because of the rock's dampness, and turned around to look at him. The young man also belonged to the same moment in time as she did. He belonged to the same sparkling moment in time and was just a part of that tiny and enormous everything that surrounded them. He turned to look at her, recognized her, and tried not to smile. They did not need to comfort one another. They were one and the same person.

Ric's voice pulled them out of their stupor. He and Manfred were leading her daughter by the hand. It was five-thirty. Klaus and Ernst walked behind them. They were all together. Only Siegfried was missing. Barbara was surprised. She stared at all of them.

"Where's Siegfried?" the young girl asked.

Her mother and her friends said nothing. A little later they all went out to look for him. They swam in all directions, searched all the rocks, and when night fell, they returned to the prison. Barbara and her daughter accompanied them there. They needed to testify that he could not have escaped. On the table of their hotel room, Barbara found the letter in which she should have explained to the young man why they could not see each other again.

On the train, someone asked the young girl: "Why is your sister so sad?"

Barbara knew that her mother was not the only sad one; she too would search for the green uniform in the reflections of the train window and search for him later on the beaches, on the streets, in the windows of her house. She had lost her first love.

LOOK FOR MY OBITUARY

THE YOUNG WOMAN ran down the street, indifferent to the rain and the night's emptiness. In her rush to escape, she forgot to shut the gates of her house. Her shoes pounded on the asphalt as if knocking on the rainy night. She turned the corner, slowed down, gazed at the treetops bending in the wind; she buttoned her raincoat and kept on going. She walked straight ahead, as if she knew exactly where she was heading, though this really was not the case. She wasn't afraid. The streets, empty at this time of night, only offered graceful trees swaying in the rain and chrysanthemums that illuminated the shadows like tiny smothered suns. No one was around; she alone walked rapidly on the narrow, slippery sidewalks... She walked a long while absorbed in herself, trying hard not to cry; it was better for her to look ahead at the rain saturating her face and hair. "He who loves the rain loves poetry," a Japanese gardener had once told her. She remembered her parted brows and her eyes painted to resemble swallow wings, and since it was absolutely forbidden, she decided to steal a huge bunch of chrysanthemums from the planters and the gardens. She was just about to steal them when she spied a man in short sleeves watching her from under a young oak tree. She realized he was just a few steps from her. She saw that he had dark, shiny eyes—Indian eyes—and knew that he would accost her as soon as she went by him. Her fear made her seemingly calm; she continued walking, past the tree, and glanced at the man in shirt sleeves who, in turn, refused to take his eyes off her. She had forgotten her desire to steal the chrysanthemums. She sensed that the minute she passed him the man would start to follow her. She walked erect, aware of the street's emptiness and the futility of calling for help. The windows beyond the flower beds were all darkened. She had barely walked a few feet past him when she felt that the man had abandoned his hiding place and was now trailing her. She imagined him calm, walking with his hands in his pants pockets, following her with the sureness of someone who knows just when to catch up to her. She turned at the first corner, hoping to lose him, and picked up her pace. Her heart was beating so loudly that she could not hear which way the stranger was going. A few seconds later, the man's footsteps turned the corner. As soon as the young girl heard him, she picked up speed; she heard the man walking faster as well. The street suddenly seemed full of hurried footsteps. The girl turned the following corner and began running, open-mouthed, feeling both the rain and the wind gagging her. Her running split the night like the rattle of a machine gun. Behind her, the man's strides pounded the asphalt. She didn't recognize the dark street she was on, full of towering streetlights set far apart, giving the shadows strange violet reflections. It was a long, slightly curving street; low houses lined one side of it, and it seemed as if the other side was bounded by the edge of a small forest. All of a sudden she knew she had entered the perfect place for a crime to be committed.

A little farther, beyond the curve in the road and half-hidden by treetops and the unevenness of the land, she saw rising—as in the stories she had read as a child—the glowing windows of a small house behind a dark nineteenth century gate. She ran toward the lights, but was momentarily stopped by a sudden deafening flash of lights and whistles; she saw the wooden barriers of a railroad crossing going down. She reached the barriers and, without a moment's hesitation, crossed the tracks before the train arrived, and threw herself against the house gates.

"Help!...Help!...Please open up!...Please..." she shouted gripping the thick black iron bars of the gate. The train appeared behind her, unaware that anything was wrong since it made its own commotion. The man in shirt-sleeves was caught behind the tracks, the passing freight cars hiding him from view. But the train passed quickly, and the long row of red cars would soon come to an end. No one in the house responded to her cries for help.

She turned around hopelessly and found herself beside a car waiting for the train to pass. She instantly let go of the house gates, came over to the car, opened the passenger door and got in. The driver looked at her in surprise.

"Help me!" the young girl screamed, clasping him around the neck.

Shocked, Miguel tried to escape her embrace.

"What's wrong?"

The young woman dropped her head into his shoulders and clung to his arm.

"He wants to kill me!"

"Who does?"

The woman lifted her head and turned around to look at the train that just that minute disappeared. Beyond the train's last car the silent street could be seen.

"That man!" the young girl screamed, pointing to a spot on the other side of the tracks.

No one stood at the spot she indicated. The man in shirt-sleeves had disappeared and the winding, empty street was clear. Miguel stared at the emptiness stirred only by the rain and then glanced at the lit-up houses and finally at her, suspiciously.

"There's no one there," he said, calmly.

"He's there, hiding, waiting for me," she insisted. She was aware that the man didn't believe her.

"Go back home," he said quietly.

"I don't want to! Take me far away from here. He is going to come up and stab us in the back."

"Who?" he asked, growing irritated.

"Him!"

"Listen, sweetie. Take it easy," Miguel answered, about to step out of his car.

The young woman threw herself upon him and held him tightly. "Please...let's drive off," she begged, without letting go.

Miguel looked at her sceptically. She was pretty with her long blond hair soaked through by the rain. He noticed that she was wearing only a very short nightgown under her raincoat. He had the impression that she was either crazy or on drugs.

"Please, let's go!" the young girl cried.

Miguel obeyed and drove off. She immediately seemed more at ease and sat back in her seat without saying a word.

"Why did you run away?" he asked in a conciliatory tone. He tried laying a hand on the young woman's bare knee.

Upon seeing this bold gesture, the young woman sat further back in her seat and crossed her legs. Why did this stranger feel he had the right to touch her legs? She watched the rainy night attentively through the windshield and said nothing. Miguel looked into her eyes suspiciously and noticed her hostile attitude. "What's this all about? Is she trying to get me mixed up in something shady?" he asked himself. The lonely figure of a policeman walking his beat emerged from the depths of the night.

"I wonder if this policeman can help figure this out," Miguel said casually, watching her from the corner of his eyes.

The young woman seemed more scared, but decided to keep quiet while Miguel drove the car toward the policeman. She lowered her eyes spitefully while he stopped the car. The officer approached courteously, glad to have someone to talk to during his solitary rounds. He too was frightened going around on his bicycle, waiting for some killer who might jump him from behind.

"Is something wrong, mister?" he asked.

Miguel looked at the officer's kind eyes and then sneaked a quick look at the girl who had lowered her head submissively. For a few seconds he didn't know what to do next. His unexpected passenger seemed suddenly so defenseless.

"We're a bit lost..." he said, asking for the way to x street.

The officer threw himself into a detailed explanation that neither Miguel nor the young woman heard, but he kept right on talking, glad to have some company.

"Thanks, thanks a lot."

The policeman returned to his solitary rounds while they headed off as fast as they could. They drove in no set direction, in silence, each one lost in his own thoughts.

"You're a kind man," she said shyly.

"There's nothing kind about me."

He drove the car toward Reforma Boulevard, circled around the *Fuente de Petróleos* and continued toward the center of town.

"I can get out here. This area's pretty well-lit..."

Miguel looked at her with resentment; now he didn't want the young girl to leave him. He pretended he hadn't heard her, but she insisted on getting out, somewhere near the *San Juan de Letrán* market.

"Where can I drop you off?" he asked, sure of himself.

"I really don't know...It's the first time I don't know where I want to go," she answered.

"What about your house?" he asked harshly.

The girl snapped her fingers, looked right at him and said simple-mindedly: "It's disappeared!"

Miguel stopped the car and stared at his passenger. He looked carefully at her bare legs, her feet slipped into some old moccasins and her hands rigorously crossed over her buttoned raincoat. She was determined not to listen to him. She put on a dignified but stubborn look. Her expression seemed closed off to any kind of discussion, and a few tufts of hair fell over her forehead. Something had happened while the young woman slept, something had awakened her and made her flee. He tried to read her face for some kind of clue to her flight and her serious attitude. He decided to smile and ran a hand over her rain-soaked hair.

"Some quarrel?"

She shook her head and angrily wiped away the tears that ran down her face.

"A death," she answered angrily.

"A death?" he asked in shock, holding her face so that she would have to look at him.

"Yes, my own death," she answered, without hesitating.

The young woman's words terrified him; he didn't know what to say. He remained pensive and quiet. Had someone tried to kill her?

"Does it seem strange to you?" she asked quite openly.

"Well, no, but..."

Why was he lying when he found not only the girl but the whole situation quite strange? Perhaps he lied to awaken the trust of his bizarre companion. He looked at her

worriedly and, just to do something, he took out his hand-
kerchief and wiped the damp streaks on her face left by the
recent tears.

"What am I supposed to do with you?" he asked in all
honesty.

"Let's go get a cup of coffee. I'm feeling chilled."

Without thinking, she lifted her legs onto the seat and
rested her head on Miguel's lap.

"This way no one will see me and I'll be able to see the
passing treetops," she said calmly.

"But I can't drive like that," he was about to say. Instead,
he lowered his eyes to gaze upon the trusting face of the
mysterious girl. He heard her say: "This way I'm not scared."

Miguel gave in. An odd emotion had seized his heart
and he slowed down the car just to be able to look at her.

"You look like someone who drowned...very beautiful,"
he whispered.

She shut her eyes, then opened them again and looked
up at him.

"It's true...I'm not of this world. It just wasn't worth it
to go on living," answered the young girl, watching the
windshield battered by the rain. Small streams of water ran
down the glass, forming a pattern of rapidly flowing canals
racing dizzily.

"You're also not of this world. Both of us are at the
bottom of a river," she added, as she raised her hand and
caressed his on the steering wheel.

The man said nothing. He decided not to look at her as
she lay on his lap, with her eyes watching the rain and a
world so different from his opening up between the bursts
of water that enveloped the car.

"I didn't know that I would drown with someone as
nice as you—" she said, kissing her fingertips and then
touching his as if transmitting the kiss to them.

Miguel still said nothing; he was in no rush. Where was he going? Bewitched by the unanticipated events, he allowed himself to drive down any street. He lowered his eyes and watched the young woman who rested her head on his lap. She was peaceful, as if she had always traveled supported by him. Miguel was suddenly frightened. The young woman seemed so familiar that it was hard to believe that he had met her just a few minutes earlier. He glanced at her, preoccupied. "You know something? I know you..."

She looked back at him calmly. "I know you, too."

Miguel stopped the car, bent over the steering wheel, and silently tried to search his mind for the place where he had first met her. He glanced back at her and said in all seriousness: "Where did we first see each other?"

"Before coming to this world, and that's why we are now leaving it together."

Lost in thought, he stroked the woman's hair as it fell haphazardly over his cashmere pants.

"And we never saw each other in this world?"

"No, never!" she answered, closing her eyes, sure of her words.

"That's very sad."

Miguel stroked her eyelids, soft and tender as the petals of a camellia.

"Did you live a sad life?" she asked, letting him caress her.

"I was yearning for you...looking for you. I had every-thing, but you. What about yourself?"

"I have this night."

Miguel lifted her, pressed her against his chest. Outside the rain kept beating down against the windshield.

"Why, you're freezing!"

He laid her back down on his lap and drove off again looking for a coffee shop. "For my beautiful drowned woman," he said to himself, not looking at her. He stopped the car at a coffee shop in *Las Lomas*. He glanced at the young girl, realized that the world had become so unreal now.

"Let's go have our cup of coffee," he said gently.

"I can't go out...I'm scared that someone will see me...That would be awful..." she answered.

He watched her slip off his lap and hide herself on the floor of the car, all curled up.

"I want you to bring me the coffee," she asked softly.

He wasn't surprised at her request. Without thinking, he was becoming used to her eccentricities. She must be in quite a jam. He went into the shop alone and came out, a few minutes later, coffee in hand. The young woman drank it in small sips in her hiding place. He wanted to ask her why she hid herself so, what was she so afraid of, but since he knew she would not tell him the truth, he didn't bother to ask.

The streetlights barely reached the dark corner of the car where the woman hid. She returned the empty cup to him, and he stroked her head.

"What was your other life like?" he asked.

The woman made a face, but said nothing.

"Do you prefer this one?" he asked shyly.

The woman kissed the hand stroking her hair; she stayed still on the floor of the car. Miguel went back into the cafe, paid the bill, and came back to her; he wanted to leave at once. He drove off with no direction in mind, feeling confused. He vaguely understood that this wasn't to be just a simple affair; every once in a while he glanced at his companion, who had once more put her head on his lap and calmly gazed at the sky patterned by bursts of rain.

He found himself driving to the outskirts of Tacubaya. He stopped the car on a dark little street; everyone was asleep at that hour, no one walked through the darkness. The night had turned lonely and silent.

"Come, my little one."

He took her in his arms to kiss her; seconds later, a muted flashlight lit up their embrace. The terrified girl pulled away and covered her face with her hands. A policeman appeared.

"Is there a problem?" he asked.

"No, officer..."

"Get going then," he said, flashing his light inside of the car.

"Not allowed to kiss you on the street," Miguel laughed, and he started driving off.

"Not allowed to love me in this world," the young girl answered.

They drove around a bit, not knowing where to go; they passed by motels, neon signs announcing hourly rates. Miguel didn't dare suggest going to one. "It would cheapen the night," he said to himself, disgusted by his vulgar thoughts. He decided to take the highway to Cuernavaca; from there they could look down on the city. Through the rain and shadows at the bottom rim of the sky, a radiance began to develop like a light green streak that was trying to open a way through the dark storm. Even the old houses started taking on new shapes.

"Ghosts begin to vanish around this time of night," the young woman said gloomily.

Her companion was startled. She bent her head. She was no longer lying across his lap; she was once more sitting up in a dignified posture, with her arms crossed on her raincoat. For the first time, Miguel realized how young she was; at most twenty-two, almost a mere teenager, and he felt old at her side. He observed her good manners which indicated a strict upbringing, and listened to her silence.

"You're not going to disappear. I want to love you, always love you," he claimed.

"I should go. It was only a dream."

They had stopped at a highway lookout; the rain had mysteriously stopped falling and the air was fresh, newly born. Below them the city spread out, taking on pale hues. A few firecrackers tore at the morning sky. With their elbows on the stone railing, they watched the roman candles as they shot up into the sky with a strange energy, only to cascade into orange lights that fell like a new rain of fire over the city. An old memory, an inexplicable sorrow overtook him and he remembered his childhood and the old balcony of his boyhood room.

"Let's go," the girl said.

They went back to the city. Once more they found themselves in Tacubaya.

"I'll look for a taxi," the girl said softly.

Miguel's hand held her back.

"Where can I see you?" he asked, hardly looking at her.

"In heaven, today, tomorrow, whenever..."

Miguel let go of her to pull out his address book; he ripped out a page and wrote his name and phone number on it.

"Call me, please," he said, handing her the paper.

The girl put the paper away in a pocket of the raincoat, looked strangely at her friend and dashed off. Miguel ran after her, screaming "I'll take you!"

"No! ...it's better for me to go alone..."

A taxi appeared and she ran toward it, gesturing with her arms in the air. Miguel stopped running, half in shock, and only managed to shout: "What's your name?"

"Irene..." she answered, about to get into the cab.

"If you don't call me, I'll come looking for you," he shouted adamantly.

He saw her climb into the cab which drove off quickly. Its place remained empty, as happens when a miracle takes place: waiting for the unexpected event to repeat itself in the knowledge that the miracle will never again occur... Feeling crushed, Miguel climbed back in his car and rested his chin on the steering wheel, with eyes fixed on the sky full of fireworks, trying in vain to reconstruct the past and remember his present life. What was his present life? Irene! He associated her name with the sea and with the police cars when they travel across the city, sirens whining, indicating a serious, unseen danger for the pedestrians who are frightened as they pass by. "Irene, Selene, Sirena," he said, mechanically to himself, and he knew he was in danger.

He was not at all interested in what was going on around him. A coffee shop opened its doors and he remembered that he had to go home. He reluctantly started up his car, drove to *Las Lomas* and stopped at the house next to the railroad tracks where the night before he had found Irene. "She must be home by now," he told himself. He parked the car in front of the house, which dated back to the turn of the century. The black-painted iron fence, the yard full of old trees, the rose bushes and the gravel road to the small staircase that led to the entrance terrace—all of it belonged to that era. At the left side of the house there stood a small tower whose windows were covered with thin white curtains. The air around the house set at the back of the garden was peaceful and aromatic. The house was encased in silence, lost in that unexpected place, and, together with the grounds, completely in its own world. It was just like Irene: mysterious and poetic. The quiet of the place intimidated him; he could not knock on the door at that hour. Irene could turn angry at his impropriety. The tower's thin curtains seemed to shift slightly and he was sure that someone was spying on him: maybe it was Irene herself. He started up the car and drove away slowly, glancing back several times.

When he reached his street, morning shone on the trees washed by the rain; the clock on the dashboard marked eight. Miguel slowed down. He had no desire to go home— he needed to get a grip on his own feelings first. Without realizing it, he found himself in front of his house, separated from the street by a high wall and a huge gate that opened automatically when the remote was activated. "I live in a prison," he thought. He pressed on the horn and the gate opened from inside.

"Good morning, sir," said the guard, unctuously.

He crossed the foyer of his house like a sleepwalker. He had to talk to his wife; he wondered if he could bear her nagging. He remembered the thick air, packed with perfumes, powders, and cosmetics floating in her huge bedroom. As usual, the curtains would be drawn and for sure she would be sick. Enriqueta was a complainer, and now she'd be indignant—he didn't think he could face her. "I can't do it," he told himself, and walked by the closed door of his wife's bedroom. Why had he gotten married? He was the victim of a lethal fate. He knew it from the moment his mother had insisted on a marriage of reason and convenience. "Marriage is a social rite; love is something that ends...What else do you want? Enriqueta is a sweet girl, pretty and brought up right," she had told him time and again. His mother was afraid that he would do something stupid like marry a loose woman or one from the lower classes—

The sudden appearance of his two sons surprised him. He had forgotten about them. Nine-year-old Miguelito and his brother Enrique glared at him.

"Mommy's sick..." Miguelito said, not giving him a kiss.

Their nanny took them by the hand to bring them to their grandmother's house; Miguel felt relief when he saw them leave with the woman. His marriage was composed of small annoyances and personal attacks which he had tried to ignore. His sons compensated for his everyday disappointments, but now not even their presence could relieve him of the painful feeling that had seized him.

He heard Enriqueta's voice: "Come in, Lupe..."

His wife pretended to have confused his footsteps with those of her personal maid; Miguel had no choice but to retrace his steps and go into Enriqueta's room. He found her wearing a lace dressing gown, lying in bed, her head resting on huge pillows. Her lids were half-closed and puffy now from her recent tears. He didn't know what to say. The perfumed scent in the room made him nauseated. He wanted to open the balcony windows to let in the fresh morning air, washed by the rains of the night before. The summer storm had worked miracles but at that moment, it was as remote and as irretrievable as his own childhood.

Irene, saturated by the rain, had dissolved into the morning light; all that was left was an enclosed room reeking of perfume. He dropped into a blue silk chair and saw his reflection in the antique mirror; that was him: a tragic expression and a face tanned by the sun.

"Something unexpected came up..." he said, rather honestly.

"Sorry, but I don't feel well...I woke up with a splitting headache..." Enriqueta answered, trying to avoid looking at him. Miguel annoyed her. At that moment she hated his muscular body and his athletic hands, so tanned and healthy. She thought she saw a new flicker in his lucid eyes. "He doesn't look like a married man..." she said resentfully to herself.

Miguel stood in front of her, but he was somewhere else,

far away from this room and this house. She felt deeply humiliated. "Some cheap whore..." she thought, irritated.

Neither of them said a thing. Actually, they had said everything there was to say in the ten years they had been married. "He's never said that he loves me," she said angrily.

Miguel, for his part, wondered nervously what had been said to Irene at home regarding her evening escapade. "We shouldn't have come back; we should have driven down any highway and just disappeared," he thought, feeling terribly unhappy.

"Remember this?" Enriqueta asked nervously.

As she said it, she unfurled an elegant scroll with the Presidential Seal. Miguel came closer and curiously examined the invitation. He remembered the fireworks that had lit up the Mexican sky the night before and smiled joyfully: it was September 15th.

"Ah, Independence Day..." he said aloud.

His wife looked at his powerful hands, his wide shoulders and felt that primitive hatred of him returning. No doubt he had spent the night making love to a woman and she had to wait for him at home, admire his physique from afar. Day by day Miguel seemed more of a stranger.

"I want to take a nap..." she heard him say.

Without further explanation, he stepped out of his wife's room and went to his room at the farthest point of that wing of the house. He vainly tried to sleep; the image of Irene wrapped up in her rain-soaked raincoat appeared whenever he closed his eyes. "She must call me," he repeated to himself a thousand times.

At night, wearing a smoking jacket, he patiently waited for his wife, who always took a long time putting on her make-up. He smoked a few cigarettes and gazed out, with little feeling, at the elegant entrance of his house. He heard the phone ring and rushed to his study, but someone, surely his wife, had answered first. He managed to hear her say: "I'm the lady of the house." He angrily sat down in a chair. A few minutes later Enriqueta appeared wearing an evening gown. He disliked her diamonds and her bouffant hairstyle. She awaited a compliment that she did not get. Suddenly everything had become so strange to Miguel: that woman who was his wife, the now inhospitable house, the servants, his study.

"No one's called me?" he asked.

"No one!" she said triumphantly.

A servant opened the door. They got into the car, both in a venomous mood. Miguel glanced at her every now and then, surprised that Irene was not sitting in her place. Enriqueta also watched him out of the corner of her eyes. Her husband's aloofness deeply humiliated her. She knew that something irrevocable had occurred, but she decided not to talk to him. Miguel did not head downtown, but instead drove toward Irene's house.

"Let's get some fresh air before going to shut ourselves up at the party. Besides we're a little early," he said decisively.

She had guessed his uneasiness and now glanced at him with displeasure. They drove past the house by the railroad tracks; it was like the night before, lights on, peaceful, cut off from the world, in a kind of poetic existence. Miguel retained his air of indifference, and his wife was not aware of anything but that her husband seemed fidgety and miserable.

They drove back to Reforma Boulevard, magnificently illuminated. The Diana Fountain was ablaze with lights like a multicolored fire. Those in the Independence Day parade laughed with excitement; they carried tricolored flags in their hands and wore costume hats on their heads. Down the whole stretch of the boulevard there was an endless line of cars, like theirs, bound for the Zócalo; the sidewalks were jammed with people, toy and candy stands, masked revelers, "spook-the-in-laws" toys, whistle-blowing and laughter.

Miguel drove slowly toward the National Palace. He said nothing, Enriqueta looked at him angrily—he seemed to be searching for someone. Finally he decided to join the procession of official cars that moved in slow and orderly fashion toward the Palace. Miguel thought that in one car he had seen Irene's rigid figure and her now bare shoulders. She had a stubborn look on her face and he knew her hands were crossed on the folds of her silk skirt. He jerked the car out of the line to try and catch the car with the young woman, but a traffic cop stopped him dead and approached the side to rebuke him. Annoyed, he had to wait for a hole in the slow-moving line to rejoin the procession.

"Are you crazy?" Enriqueta asked him angrily.

"Don't doubt it..."

The Zócalo was crammed with a dark crowd that moved like one huge animal. When they got out of the car, the throng pushed to admire the elegant couple going to the party. They went in, helped by guards, and reached the marble staircase. Miguel wanted to ignore the solemn attendants and rush in to find Irene, but Enriqueta, aware of the sumptuous folds of her dress, obliged him to walk slowly up the steps. Once inside the huge rooms, Miguel looked hopelessly for the young woman. "How silly, so silly; it wasn't her," he repeated, as he remembered the house close to the train tracks.

He found himself surrounded by people indifferent to his suffering. He coldly surveyed the guests, looking only for her and not noticing that several people greeted him with nods. Enriqueta pulled him back to a group of friends who ridiculed Miguel's confusion.

"Sorry, so sorry, I'm a bit distracted..." he said restlessly, without slowing his inspection of the guests to see if he could find Irene's face. Suddenly he thought he saw her in the back of the room, but just as quickly other heads blocked his view.

"I'll be right back..."

He walked straight over to where he thought he had seen her. His wife caught up with him.

She was indignant. "What are you up to?"

Miguel looked at her submissively. What could he say to her? Nothing. He felt powerless—his friends stared at him—and ridiculous in the center of that luxurious room filled by elegant men and bejeweled women.

"I told you this morning that I felt sick...I'd prefer to go home..." said Enriqueta.

He tried to apologize, but she insisted that they leave the party immediately. He heard her voice while his mind wandered to other memories of the 15th of September. Once more he felt the same bitter yearning, the same longing for the tears of that lost childhood night. His wife shattered his thoughts to insist that they leave at once. Giving in, he found himself leaving the National Palace and in his car on the way home. They drove back in silence.

"It would be better if you started your holidays earlier. Why wait?" he asked, as they reached their house.

"I don't want to change my plans," she said brusquely.

Miguel had a bad night, smoking one cigarette after the other. Irene had cast a spell on him: had it really been her, first in the car and then later at the party? "I'll go to her house tomorrow," he told himself, as he fell asleep almost at daybreak.

The new day found him restless; he passed by his wife's bedroom door and rushed into the street. At his office he tried to handle certain matters that barely a few hours earlier had absorbed him. Around noon, he got into his car and drove off toward *Las Lomas*. Feeling peaceful, he parked the car in front of the old gates of the house and once more surveyed the garden, the terrace, and the small slate-roofed tower. The house itself was under a unique spell; he felt that he would never be able to break it, and so he got out of the car and rang the bell. No one answered. He glanced around in surprise and once again rang, only more strongly this time. The ringing seemed to have scared the birds, and they now flocked from one treetop to another. Miguel saw a hand slowly parting the curtains of the glass doors that opened onto the terrace. He found that encouraging and once again rang. The door half-opened and he saw a little old lady with her hair up in a bun and an embroidered collar. Miguel signaled for her to come closer. The woman just closed the door. "She went to get Irene," he said to himself and he waited a few minutes grasping the bars of the gate. But realizing that the whole house had returned to its normal quiet, he again rang so hard that he himself thought he was being rude. His action drew results; the door opened again and the same lady appeared on the terrace. He smiled happily and raised a hand to greet her. The old woman walked across the terrace, down the stone steps and slowly walked the gravel path that led to the gate. The old woman seemed surprised by the insistence of the elegant and good-looking young man.

"Can I help you, sir?" she asked faintly.

"Yes. Excuse me, but I need to speak with Miss Irene for a second..."

He stopped short, certain that someone in the tower was watching him. He quickly looked up and saw the thin white curtain close at a window, hiding a shadowy form which he was sure was that of a female.

"With whom?" asked the old woman, acting as if she couldn't hear very well.

"With Miss Irene..." he repeated.

The old woman looked at him in shock, as if he had said something improper.

"Maybe I should've said Mrs..." he said to himself, worried. She opened her mouth to say something, but decided not to. She carefully looked him over and then glanced at the car parked in front of the house.

"Just a second. Let me ask," she said with that same, almost extinguished, voice.

Miguel watched her shuffle away, climb the steps, cross the terrace and go inside, closing the door behind her. The shadowy form in the tower had disappeared, and Miguel decided to wait, leaning on the gate.

Inside the house, Miss Rosalia met with her younger sister Clementina who had come down from the tower and now eagerly awaited the news.

"I'm sure of it, it's the same car that stopped here night before last when that young woman who returned yesterday morning caused such a stir—"

"How awful! Was he the one who kidnapped her?" asked a terrified Clementina.

"I'm not sure...he seems so polite. He has blue eyes, but now everything's different..."

"Don't go back out. This is a dangerous situation...Do you think he's a policeman?"

"A policeman? No, he's too well-dressed for that..."

"Then maybe he's a criminal, Rosalia. You have to be very careful not to challenge him; remember what we've learned on television."

"Yes, I'll be careful. God help me! Either a policeman or a criminal at our house!" Rosalia exclaimed, terrified.

The two sisters kept absolutely quiet and on tiptoe went up to the tower to observe the visitor. From there they could see him ringing, waiting, leaning on the gate, shooting longing glances at the terrace door.

"He asked for her. Her name is Irene...Look at him, he seems so sad!" Rosalia said.

"He wants to know if we suspect something...Poor man! Something's wrong with him..." Clementina whispered.

Half an hour later they saw him climb into his car; he looked out on the house, with sorrowful eyes, leaning on the steering wheel.

"We can't do anything for him," said Rosalia, trying to console herself from the worry that the stranger made her feel.

"Nothing! We'd better not get mixed up in this shady affair," her sister agreed, sharing the pity her sister felt for the young man in the car.

"Is Irene alive?"

"I hope so! God knows, with these young women today—" breathed Clementina.

Miguel waited in vain for over an hour and a half. Could Irene be married? The old woman's shock hadn't seemed fake. It was silly to keep guard on the house, though it was repugnant to leave this place and go back to the routine of life without speaking to Irene. Defeated by the silence, he left a short message. "Please call me," he wrote on a page from his appointment book; he then ripped it out, got out of the car, and tossed the note through the bars. Then he slowly left to rejoin Enriqueta.

He had hardly driven off when Rosalia carefully sneaked out to get the piece of paper that had nearly been carried off by the afternoon wind, a harbinger of a storm. The two sisters read the note several times.

"Who does he want to call him?" Clementina asked worriedly.

"Irene. That's why he came to look for her."

"Hadn't he driven off with her?"

"Maybe she escaped again...you know what? He's in love!" Rosalia said victoriously.

"With whom?...And why is he looking for her in our house?" Clementina asked, astonished.

"Well, anything's better than calling the police. We will pretend that we know nothing..." Rosalia asserted. The two sisters sighed deeply and waited quietly for new developments.

For Miguel, life resumed its usual pattern: he ate dinner with Enriqueta and some boisterous friends in popular restaurants. He had no interest in conversing, and so glanced at the nearby tables for Irene's lost face. He looked for her also in the streets or in movie lines, always repeating: "She's no good, she doesn't call me." He preferred the silence in his office; there, at least, he could reflect on his obsessions without having to pretend as he did with his wife or his friends. Every once in a while he would drive by the house with the tower hoping to get a glimpse of the young woman. At times he would stop before the gates for a few minutes, but he did not see either the young girl nor the kind old woman who had come out to meet him.

"There he is again..." said Clementina, alarmed.

Rosalia would hurry to gaze through the muslin curtains; it wasn't normal for that stranger to drive around their house just for his pleasure. His presence was part of something important, some pressing affair that the sisters knew nothing about. Seven days had passed since that young woman had clung to the gate, letting out sharp cries for help; then she had escaped in that late model car which parked at all hours of the day or night in front of their garden.

"It's something we can never hope to understand..." they said, as the car drove off.

"I don't understand this obsession...she's an adventuress..." Miguel said to himself, as he raised his glass at the baptism of his brother's son. He sought out Enriqueta, who was chatting amiably with his sister-in-law. His mother was right: his wife was sweet and had perfect manners. He almost felt regret, but then a servant came over to him and almost whispered into his ear: "Sir, there's a call for you."

Miguel almost tiptoed over to his brother's study. Who could be calling him at that moment?

"Miguel, I'm calling from a sound booth in Casa Wagner on Venustiano Carranza Street. Come quickly," said Irene in a calm voice.

Stunned he heard the receiver click; he looked all around him, afraid that there'd be a witness to this secret talk. The party noises, the laughter, the buzz of conversation reached his ears. He stepped out of the study; no one had noticed his absence. Enriqueta was still chatting with his sister-in-law. Without giving it a second thought, he escaped to the street and got into his car.

"An emergency," he said to one of his brother's servants.

He raced across the city, which seemed enormously broad. When he was near the meeting point, he parked the car and rushed to find the young woman. Casa Wagner was the most isolated place in the world; he never would have thought of looking for his friend there. A punctilious employee walked over to him; Miguel barely glanced at him, as he searched for the music booths. Behind the glass of one booth, he saw Irene sitting, her hands folded on her knees and a serious expression on her face, listening to music he could not hear. He opened the accordion door and rushed in. Irene lifted her eyes, a blast of violins and heavenly notes carried him far away from the vulgar everyday world.

"Irene..."

"It's Mozart, Miguel..." she answered simply.

They stayed like that, looking at one another without speaking, lulled by music that expressed what they were incapable of saying. Irene wore the same raincoat and the same old moccasins. She resembled a modern, mythological character. To Miguel, she seemed to be a sea angel and he felt he was facing an unreal being, a dweller of the rain, a woman who had escaped from the sea or from the music. He looked at her in fascination and suddenly the music stopped. Irene stood up. They walked together out to the street; when he tried to put his arm around her waist, she stopped him at once.

"Take me wherever you want, but you go first and I'll follow," said the young woman, stepping back a little.

He walked apprehensively in front of her till they reached the car. He opened the door for her; she quickly got in and curled up on the floor. He drove off rapidly. Without saying a single word, Irene laid her head on his lap and stared at the roofs of the houses and later, when they were on the highway, at the tips of trees. Miguel was quiet and threw somber glances at his friend's peaceful face.

"It was Mozart...no one went to his burial, only his little dog...Would you go to mine?" Irene asked. She opened her eyes so she could look upon her friend with a fleeting look.

"Love, where do you go when I'm not with you?" Miguel asked.

"I'm with you...I follow you on the sidewalks, I go up with you to your office, I go to cafes, to parties, I spy on you and then as you now see, I call you during a baptism..." Irene said calmly.

Miguel stopped the car at the curb. He gently raised the young woman to a sitting position and looked at her as if he wanted to read her face.

"How did you know I would be at my brother's house?"

"I already told you, I spy on you..." she breathed, offering him her mouth.

"Why do they say you're not at home?" he asked, seeing her reaching out toward him with closed eyes.

"I don't know..." she answered, not changing her position.

"Who are those two old women who live in your house?" Miguel asked, gazing down on the young face still awaiting his kiss.

"My aunts..."

Miguel kissed her eyelids and took her in his arms. He felt that something more serious than the first night was happening; he wanted to tell her he was in love with her, but he just stroked her hair instead. She moved his hand away, then turning somber, she curled up in the seat, crossed her hands on her knees and without looking at him asked: "Am I your love?"

"Imagine that you are. Imagine that you are my love, that I can't live without you...the world turns to ashes when I can't see you. Furthermore, now I know it was always made of ashes..."

Irene turned to look at him; she lifted her legs onto the seat, placed her arms on the backrest and laid her head on them. She stayed thinking like that for a few seconds.

"You also are my love...What are we going to do?" she asked calmly.

Miguel hugged the steering wheel and watched the sun going down. He said nothing. Irene's question sank him into a kind of reality he preferred to eradicate.

"How can we erase the past?" he asked in agony.

"The past cannot be eliminated," she said gently.

Miguel looked at her; her words were an evil omen.

"At this moment we can change what's going to be...the two of us. Later it'll be too late," she said, a deeply sad look on her face.

"Tell me, love: what's going to be?" he asked, painfully.

Irene raised her eyes and turned to look at the sky through the windshield; it was now slowly being covered by dark layers.

"Nothing...after all, our future is there, in heaven."

"In heaven? But what about here, now, on earth..."

"Here?" Irene shot him a sad look.

"Yes, here," he asked, taking her into his arms.

"Here your past cannot be eliminated," she repeated, turning her face.

Miguel held her against his chest. What Irene said was true and yet he wanted to suggest that they run off; that it was the only way they could be together. This thought depressed him.

"You're so young and have had so little," he said, feeling guilty.

"And what do you give to a young woman?" Irene asked.

"To a young woman? Why, life! All of life!"

He pulled away from her and drove off...He didn't know what to do nor where to take the woman who was lying across his lap. In truth, that was all he needed: to run away with her down a dark highway. Run away to forget what neither one of them could forget. Perhaps in their flight they would find what both of them were looking for: to stay together forever. They drove through several lost towns. Miguel stopped the car in one.

"I'm going to take you to eat something."

The town's people watched them walk the small streets looking for a restaurant. They found a rather clean inn; progress had reached that spot and a jukebox played sentimental records. The owner, a friendly old woman, prepared their meal.

"Let's dance," Irene said.

"Dance, sir, dance with the young woman," ordered the owner, proud to have such a handsome couple in her restaurant.

The other customers watched them dance in silence, somewhat shocked. Love joined them intimately; they played out a kind of lover's ritual. Later, back at their table, they ate without appetite, staring into each other's eyes and holding hands above the table.

They went out for a walk through the village, with its half-bare mud walls, dust, and bougainvilleas. They reached the countryside, walking hand in hand, lost in thought and silence. They walked down a path; only the stars lit their steps.

"It's so quiet!" Irene said, in awe.

"Yes, just you alone pounding in the center of my chest," Miguel replied.

They did not want to leave, the field seemed to be theirs, and the town, their town. They walked arm-in-arm, peacefully, protected by an order that was theirs alone. Much later, as they drove back to the city, Irene burst out crying.

"Why are you crying if you know that I never want to part from you?" he asked, stopping the car to console her.

"Never?..Check the time," she said through her tears.

Miguel glanced at the bright clock on the dashboard; it was one in the morning. He said nothing; the hours with Irene had passed at a frightening speed. He turned to her in anguish; she now sat straight up with her face in her hands. To gain a bit more time with her, he turned off on a local road and headed further into the solitude of the countryside. After a while they found an old car parked with its lights off. An old man was beside it, holding an iron bar menacingly. Miguel slowed down and Irene ordered him to stop.

"What's up?" asked Miguel, leaning out of the window.

"I'm out of gas," the old man shouted.

"Stay here! I'll go get you a canful!" Miguel yelled back.

He turned the car around and sped off toward a gas station he had seen on the main highway.

"He seemed upset. He doesn't think we're going to help him," said Irene, moved by the solitude of that old man on a country road.

They bought a can of gas and drove back to where the stranger awaited them. They saw him from afar, sitting on a rock, resigned. The car headlights got him to jump up. Miguel stop the car a few meters away; the man did not move. Miguel got out of the car; the headlights transformed him into a huge giant and the old man did something unexpected: he started howling loudly.

"No!...No!..." he shouted fearfully and began stumbling down the road.

Without thinking, Miguel took off after him. Then he stopped, came back to Irene who had also gotten out of the car to watch in shock what was happening.

"Sir, we brought you the gas!" Miguel shouted with all his might, trying to stop the old man who was now climbing an embankment. The old man turned around.

Miguel opened his trunk and took out the can of gas; he then headed toward where the old car was parked. The man hid from sight. Terrified he watched the couple's movements from afar. He saw Miguel, always staying in the glow of the headlights, put the can down on the ground and then returned to his own car.

"I'll leave it here," he shouted..

The old man reappeared on the road, cautiously, with the iron tool in his hand.

"How much do I owe you?" he shouted back.

"Nothing!"

The man stayed rooted to the spot, not changing his expression. Miguel decided to get into his car. That's when the old man began gesturing with his arms and talking.

"Please forgive me!...Young people frighten me...They've become agitators!! anarchists!!!...Murderers!"

"You're right!" Miguel screamed back, as loud as he could. He had cupped his hands to his mouth, making a kind of megaphone, so that his voice echoed throughout the countryside.

He got back into his car and drove off, leaving the gas can on the side of the road. Then he and Irene laughed. It was awful that youngsters could create such fear. Miguel felt flattered; the old man had mistaken him for a young man, him, married with children and having just turned 32.

The dashboard clock indicated it was now two-thirty. The lateness made them suddenly sad. Irene went back to her favorite position: she stretched out on her friend's lap and remained silent. He watched her curl up, realizing that he knew nothing about her, and then he found himself identifying with the old man on the country road; Irene also frightened him.

"Irene, I know nothing about you. You keep it all secret..."

The young woman opened her eyes and sat up.

"Well, you're the only person that knows everything about me..." she said, throwing her arms around his neck and burying her face in his shoulder.

"Irene, did you go to the September 16th party?" Miguel asked, taking advantage of her vulnerability.

"Yes, I went," she answered honestly.

"With whom?"

"With you...What about yourself?"

"Me? ...I went alone."

Irene angrily pulled herself away from her friend's shoulder.

"It's late..."

"Late for what?" he asked surprised.

"Late for everything. Take me back to town so I can go off."

"You're going off again?" he asked, terrified. Irene didn't answer, lowered her head and crossed her arms. He saw the closed expression on her face and realized it was useless to talk.

"I can't go back to your house and talk to your aunts; they're very strange and look at me as if I'm a murderer. They deny your existence. I also can't look for you like a crazy man all over the city...Please tell me where and when we can see each other again!" Miguel begged, not raising his eyes.

Irene turned to look at him.

"What can we do?...Vanish together?"

Miguel turned his head and said nothing. Then he added dejectedly: "I don't know...I don't know what we are going to do...anything but lose you..."

He slowed down. The trip back seemed too short and he wanted to stretch his time with Irene. He knew that as soon as they got back to the city, the risk of losing Irene increased. While they were still in the country he could search desperately for a reason that would force her to tell him where and when they could meet again. He glanced at her lying across his lap; she was truly a precious thing to him.

"From here I can see the depths of the sky; it's much further away than the clouds," Irene said.

Miguel made out an open space in the dark blue of the night; there a hidden star must be filtering a halo of unexpected light. He turned to look at Irene bathed by that radiance, and he realized that they had both entered a new world.

"Someday we will be joined as one and we will go through that door open for us in heaven," the young woman said.

Her words annoyed him. It was easy for her to console herself with an imaginary reunion in heaven; he, on the other hand, had to return home, to be with Enriqueta who only bored him. "When I see her, it's as if sand were being thrown in my eyes," he thought, recalling the mother of his sons. "Why did I ever marry her?"

Irene's peaceful face made him angry as he realized that in a few moments that same face would be under some eyes he did not know, and the idea was unbearable. He drove faster.

"And if we died in an accident?" he asked gloomily.

Irene did not respond. She just closed her eyes and let the speed of the car lull her.

"Maybe that's how we'd be together in your sky," Miguel said sarcastically.

Neither his tone nor his attitude impressed her. She softly rubbed one of his knees and said nothing. Miguel stopped the car; he wanted to tell her that she was just any stranger, that she had entered his car like an evil omen to destroy the order in his life.

"I mean nothing to you! How many times have you trapped men in the middle of the night just to abandon them? You're just a modern adventuress...You're hateful!..A liar...A deceiver..."

Irene sat up in her seat and stared at him angrily.

"Those are not your words. I don't want to hear them,"

she suddenly screamed. She opened her door, stepped out on the highway, and began running in the darkness of night.

Irene's ill-timed escape took him by surprise; he watched her speeding off, out of range of the headlights. Scared, he got out of the car and ran after her.

"Irene!...Irene..."

His voice got lost among the trees and rocks in the fields. He slowed down; the young woman's steps on the asphalt had stopped. He saw nothing in the darkness, he continued calling her, and left the highway to go in among the trees. He called her more tenderly, scared that his own words had made her run off. He wished that the sweetness of his new words could somehow erase the dreadfulness of those he had said before, but Irene walked on silently, lost in the night. He went back to his car and drove it very slowly, using the headlights to light up the highway and its dark embankments. Several times he drove back and forth by the spot where the young woman had fled. Discouraged, he parked the car and placed his head in his hands as if about to cry. What had he done? He only wanted Irene to appear at once so he could begin to live again.

"If you would be so kind as to take me back to town, it's almost daybreak," Irene said, behind him.

He turned around and was surprised to find her curled up in the back of the car. Bending over, he lifted her from her hideout. He placed her next to him and laid her back in the seat to kiss her, but she stopped his kisses.

"It's no use, Miguel, it's no use..."

She spoke solemnly; he lifted her to gaze at her grim face. He pressed her against him, overwhelmed by the weight of the love he felt for that young, unexpected stranger. He held her away from him and looked at her.

"You won't tell me who you are and what's wrong?"

Irene shook her head no.

"I love you, Irene."

"I know that...I love you as well," she answered simply.

They drove back to town, sad and grim.

"Promise me that we will see each other today?" he asked, watching the first dim lights of daybreak.

"I promise," Irene answered sadly.

They got back to town with the first light of day.

"Where and at what time shall I meet you?" Miguel asked.

"At eleven...in front of my house..." she answered hesitantly.

Miguel stroked her hair, feeling calmer. They crossed the main thoroughfares of the town and passed a small market where fruit was being unloaded.

"I'd like some fruit, I'm thirsty..." Irene requested.

"Whatever you say, love."

He stopped the car and trustingly got out. He bought peaches, oranges and grapes, feeling euphoric. He was excited by the idea of eating fruit with Irene. With her, the smallest gesture took on magical and stirring proportions. He did not see her when he got back to the car. "She's hiding in the backseat," he said, smiling as he considered his friend's childish ways. He opened the back door, planning to surprise her with the fresh fruit he carried in his arms but his happiness turned to panic: Irene had disappeared. The car was empty. He dropped the fruit and went back to the people busy unloading the crates of fruit, indifferent to his grief. A man sitting on a box eyed him with pity.

"Forget it, mister. As soon as you left the car, she took off running."

"In which direction?" Miguel asked, tears choking his voice.

"That way...Forget her, mister. She tricked you."

Miguel ran more or less in the direction that the

merchant had indicated. His running was useless. He found no trace of his friend. He went back to the car and drove off, filled with rage. He drove across town and headed for *Las Lomas.* He stopped the car in front of the tower of the house and got out, slamming the door shut; he walked to the gate and shook the bell savagely. No one moved inside the house.

"Irene!...Irene!...," he shouted with all his might, while he continued to ring the bell angrily.

He saw the door on the terrace open up a bit and repeated his angry words: "Irene, I see you!" The door closed at once.

Inside the house, Clementina and Rosalia, in their nightgowns, looked at each other, scared to death. They lodged several chairs against the door, while they listened to the screams coming from the gate.

"Today he's very excited," Rosalia said.

"No. He's crazy," Clementina broke in.

"We've got to calm him down...poor man.."

Miguel continued shaking the bell; then he saw one of the old women put her face to a window in the tower.

"Mister..."

Miguel looked at her impatiently. Rosalia was smiling, in a conciliatory way.

"Tell her that if she doesn't come out right now, I'll tear down the house!" he shouted.

The old woman was terrified.

"She's sleeping...come back later..." she said, trying to quiet him and gain time.

"I know she's not sleeping," he said angrily.

"Yes, sir, Irene is sleeping...fast asleep...I'll give her your message later; it's not a smart thing to interrupt young people's sleep," the old woman said sweetly.

"When can I come back?" Miguel asked, defeated by the old woman's politeness.

"Well...around eleven...or better yet, at noon. Is that okay?"

Miguel thanked her, got back into his car, leaned his head on the steering wheel, and seemed to cry. Rosalia saw him from the tower; she was overcome by deep sadness. Who was this handsome, desperate young man? And who was Irene? A little while later, she saw him start the car and drive off slowly, very slowly. She went downstairs to rejoin her sister who on her own had been watching him from behind the curtain of the front door.

"I saw it all. There's something strange going on," Clementina said, feeling that she had lost her usual judgment. Like her sister, she felt confused.

"Do you think he's a lunatic?" Rosalia asked softly.

"No...both of us saw when he kidnapped that unhappy girl...What could have happened later?"

"He fell in love with her, he trusted her and then the young woman, snap!, she got away..." Rosalia concluded.

"Well figured out!...But why is he looking for her here?...Now we're really mixed up in this."

"Very much, very much so," Rosalia sighed.

"We have to play along with him, not get him excited; you yourself heard that he wanted to tear down the house."

"If it weren't for those wild threats, he would be a charming young man," Rosalia concluded.

Miguel locked himself up in his room when he got home. He dropped fully dressed on his bed, ignoring Enriqueta's woeful anger and the shock of his children.

"I have no explanation to give," he had said, when he saw his wife's expression and imploring eyes.

Enriqueta's anger reached him through the closed doors of his room, but he lay motionless staring at the ceiling and, from time to time, he glanced at his wristwatch, which had stopped working. He smoked one cigarette after the next till it was the time agreed upon with Irene's aunt. He leaped up and, without saying a word, went back outside and got into his car. At eleven on the dot he was parked in front of the towered house. He looked lovingly at the train tracks and then softly rang the bell. He hadn't shaven, and he wore the same, now wrinkled, suit.

Rosalia opened the terrace door; she was elegantly dressed as if about to meet an important guest. She walked down the steps ceremoniously and strolled along the gravel path smiling. Her cordial demeanor comforted Miguel; it seemed that now he was going to get Irene back.

"Good morning, sir."

"Good morning...Sorry for this morning...What did she say?...Will she see me?"

Rosalia apologetically lowered her eyes, wrung her hands gently. Miguel saw that her lips trembled and waited in anguish.

"She didn't tell you?" she asked, eyes lowered.

"No, she didn't say anything...What's going on?" he asked anxiously.

"Sir...Irene had to go on a trip...It was a last minute thing..."

She couldn't continue. Miguel's terrified eyes cut off the speech she had prepared.

"On a trip?...Where?..."

The old woman did not respond. She had been caught off balance.

"To where?" Miguel asked, in a menacing voice.

"To Washington...that's life...things suddenly come up, without your wanting them to...and the world continues spinning..."she said in a rush, her voice trembling.

Miguel put his head in his hands; the old woman had the impression that she had killed him.

"To Washington?...How could she do that to me?" he sobbed.

"Sir...sir...don't worry...Irene will be back in a few days... I promise to let you know as soon as she returns..."

"You would promise me that?"

"I promise you. I myself will tell you, on the very day she returns...if you'd like..."

Miguel took out his appointment book, tore out a page and wrote down his name and number while he repeated over and over, in disbelief: "To Washington...To Washington..."

He gave the old woman the page; she grabbed it quickly.

"You promise that as soon as she arrives you'll let me know?" he repeated, disheartened.

"Yes, I promise."

Miguel thanked her several times, said goodbye, went back to his car and drove off slowly. Rosalia watched him leave and returned to her house, walking with difficulty. Her sister waited for her behind the curtains.

"Love is a very sad affliction, Clementina, very sad..." Rosalia said.

Miguel wandered aimlessly through his house; in the afternoon, he went to the office and hunkered down. He didn't want to go on living. The world had been torn to shreds, and he felt that the people in it were dead. He asked his secretary to get him the schedule of flights to Washington, and he studied it carefully; then he forgot about planning his trip and let hopelessness take over. "All I can do is wait."

At home he tried to avoid Enriqueta, who didn't miss a chance to pick at him for deserting her at his nephew's baptism. At night, locked in his study, he thought about the huge world just outside his room spinning around indifferently. His inner pain kept him from getting together with friends and going to the last parties of summer. The telephone's ring startled him, but it was never Irene, and the old woman had also forgotten him. The servants looked at him with pity; only they seemed to share in part the pain that paralyzed him.

One evening a servant said to him: "There's a phone call for you."

Trembling, he rushed to get it.

"Sir, it's Miss Rosalia," said a trembling voice that he recognized at once.

"Oh, yes, what's new?"

"Well, we got a letter from Irene. She says that she's sad, very sad, and that she'll be back soon..."

"When?" he asked anxiously.

"In a matter of weeks...it seems...Be patient, don't do anything foolish...Goodbye, sir."

"All right, I'll wait," he said, consoled.

Enriqueta walked by without looking at him. Miguel went down the stairs, wanting to go outside, get away from her, since she made him feel guilty. Guilty of what? He had always been a good husband. Enriqueta acknowledged that theirs was a marriage of "convenience," planned by his mother and her parents. Why did she now behave like a woman betrayed in love? "In her own eyes," he told himself, getting into the car.

He drove fast until he was in front of Irene's house; full of hope, he observed its iron bars, its garden, its tower. In that mysterious and hidden place lived a poetic young woman, so much like her own house. The sisters observed him from their tower above the house. They needed to do something to calm the wretched man...

For three days the phone did not ring for him once. On

the fourth day, at sunset, the old woman called to say that soon he would be surprised.

"Have faith, sir, have faith," Rosalia repeated.

He told himself the same words: "Have faith, have faith." They had been having dinner when he got up from the table to answer the phone. He felt hopeful now, and smiled at his wife. Then the maid said again: "There's another call for you, sir."

Enriqueta looked at him disapproving; the maid said nothing. Miguel glanced at them one at a time, threw down his napkin and left the dining room. He went to the furthest phone.

"It's me, Miguel..." Irene's voice trembled.

Miguel was so excited he could not speak.

"I'll meet you at the station, in the waiting room," said Irene, in a child's voice.

"Did you just arrive?"

"No, I'm about to leave..." and she hung up.

Without giving it a thought, Miguel also hung up and went outside; he climbed into his car and raced off. When he reached the station, he peered around anxiously till he saw her in the distance: she wore the same raincoat and was standing there, deeply engrossed in reading an American magazine. When he reached her, he took her in his arms without saying a word, kissed her over and over, as if his life depended on her lips. Irene returned his embrace, but then breathlessly begged him: "No, don't. Someone will see us..."

Miguel dragged her out of the station, toward his car; they got in and drove off very rapidly. They were carried away, unable to talk. Irene lay down across his lap and closed her eyes, as if having found peace.

"Why did you say you were leaving?" he asked resentfully.

"Because it's true, I'm leaving..." she said very softly.

"You're going nowhere! Or you're going with me...Don't you know that I can't live without you?"

"You aren't just going to live...you are going to survive death..." she said.

Miguel eagerly looked for a place where they could be alone, but the dark city seemed hostile and closed to them.

"Where can we go to talk?" he asked desperately.

He thought of going to an elegant hotel. She would go in first, get a room, then he would follow, get another room and then they would meet.

"I can't...it's dangerous if I'm seen. Anyway, the hotels are full of tourists," she said somberly.

They went to a poorer neighborhood, stopped the car and kissed. A policeman walked by and Miguel decided to drive away. Soon he was on the highway to Toluca. On the way, he looked for a turn; he went down a tree-shaded road and stopped at a fancy motel.

"No one will see you here," Miguel said softly.

Irene nodded. They met in a large room, smelling of trees, and they kissed each other like two shipwrecked people. When they awoke, they looked sadly at one another. The perfumed fields were now covered with dew, with fresh treesap. The light dropping from the sky allowed them to make out a few tender leaves on the trees.

"Irene, you know when I was still a boy, one morning I discovered in my dreams the infinite sadness of being alone in the world and I woke up crying..."

The young woman looked at him gravely, and he turned around to caress her.

"My mother came into my room and found me crying beside a window, looking at the sky lit up by fireworks. I wasn't consoled by her presence, but it almost made me feel like an orphan. 'Why are you crying?' she asked scared.

'Because of the fireworks,' I sobbed. My mother hugged me 'It's the 15th of September, don't be afraid,' she explained. But her words didn't relieve the deep, strange sorrow that came from far off. It was the same year my father died and she attributed the tears to that. 'No, I'm not crying over him,' I told her, and it was true..."

Irene moved away and threw herself face down on the bed, while he continued to take in the lost sky of his youth.

"No, it wasn't my father's death that made me feel this sharp pain. My mother could do nothing to console me, and I remained just as sad...It's something I could never cast off...Only when I'm with you do I feel cured of that pain. When I lose you, all the sadness discovered that night and built up over the years crashes down on me. That's why I can't live without you...Do you understand?...Since that morning I woke up crying for you..."

Miguel turned around to look at her. He saw her head sunk in the pillows. He came over to her, stretched out at her side and turned her face so she could see his frightened eyes.

"What's wrong, my love?"

"Nothing...mere coincidences...I was born the night of September 15th, 1940," she said, frightened.

Miguel let go of her in disbelief. He looked at her for a few seconds, took out a cigarette and smoked it, staring at her.

"My father died in 1940...It was fated that I would love you..."

It was she who now cried inconsolably.

"Don't let them kill me!" she cried, tragically.

Miguel held her to his chest.

"Kill you? ...But why?" he asked, curling her up as if she were a small child.

"For money..." Irene moaned.

"Don't say silly things," he said, smiling at her childish ways.

"Day after tomorrow you'll find my obituary in the papers..." she sobbed, hiding herself in his chest.

"Sweetheart, I'll talk to your Aunt Rosalia and fix it all up...She's a good woman!"

"Yes...she's very good," said Irene, brusquely separating herself from Miguel.

She stared at him and he felt uncomfortable.

"My dear Aunt Rosalia..." she repeated aloud, as if for herself.

"Nothing is hopeless, the past does not exist, we were both born this past September 15th...I'll tell your aunt that I'm married..." he said, nearing the window.

Irene covered her face with her hands; the sun was rising at a frightening speed. She stood up nervously.

"I'm leaving, Miguel!...I'm leaving!..." she shouted strangely.

"Why in such a rush?" he asked, startled.

"Because of my Uncle Pablo...my Uncle Pablo...If he sees me returning at such an hour...He knows nothing about the nights I've spent with you..."

"Pablo?"

Yes...the husband of my Aunt Antonieta...she's a very mean old lady..."

"Let's go. I don't want to cause you problems," he answered trustfully.

They both hurried out. They drove down the highway very rapidly, and once they were in the city, Irene begged: "It's better if I go alone...I don't want them to see me with you at this hour..."

Miguel stopped the car and they both got out to look for a taxi. Irene waited for a cab to appear with a strange expression on her face, as if she wasn't sure she wanted to go. With her eyes lowered, she played with the buttons on Miguel's shirt, with his tie, even her lover's hands; standing in front of him, she seemed to be far away.

"What's wrong, my love? Don't you want to go?" he lifted her chin and smiled.

Irene said nothing.

"Now that we love each other and will be forever together, you don't want to go? Well, don't go!" he said, feeling stirred.

Irene threw herself against him at once and kissed him deeply; then she ran across the street and climbed into an approaching taxi. From the window she saw his trusting face, watching her depart.

"If you don't call me today, I'll make a scene outside the gate of your house," he screamed, suddenly worried.

Irene waved goodbye to him.

"Look for my obituary in the papers!" she screamed just as the taxi drove off.

He heard her words feeling confused, scared; he felt stupid standing in the middle of the sidewalk. He ran to his car and, in agony, drove full speed toward Irene's house. He wanted to get there before his lover.

He found the house perfectly still as usual. He got out of the car and rang the bell. He waited a while until Miss Rosalia appeared; she seemed frightened by how early he had come. She wavered before walking down the steps, then paused halfway down the path.

"Excuse me, Miss Rosalia...You must think I'm crazy... and maybe I am...I need to see Irene..." he said mortified and without daring to admit that he had just left her in a cab.

"She's sleeping..." the old woman's voice trembled.

"She fell asleep so quickly?" he asked, giving in to his rapture.

"Yes...she's very tired...The trip, the excitement..." the old lady said softly.

"What I'm going to ask you is a bit silly, but will you please take care of her...She seemed very distraught... Everything is going to be okay," he said, blushing. He had remembered he was married, and he felt guilty in the company of that sweet, very polite old woman.

"Don't worry about it, don't worry..." she assured him, not moving a step closer.

"I'll go now. If you'd be so kind as to tell me what her plans are...later in the day..."

"Yes, don't worry, I'll take care of it," the old woman promised.

Leaning against the gate, he couldn't decide whether to stay or leave. He glanced desperately at the old woman. He wanted to confess to her that without Irene, he felt lost, but the words wouldn't flow out of his mouth and Miss Rosalia was watching him, not understanding. Finally he left the gate, got back into his car, and drove away reluctantly. He sheepishly entered his house, took a quick shower, and left for his office in a bad mood. From there, he called Irene's house.

Rosalia answered. "Irene's fine. She had breakfast. Now she's listening to the radio," the old woman explained.

"The radio?" Miguel asked, surprised.

"No, no I meant she's listening to music. That's why I can't call her..."

"I'll call later, for now just tell her that I asked after her and that I spend every second thinking about her...If she wants to, she can call me at any time," he said.

Miguel was restless, He couldn't decide whether to leave his office or not; he had to make a decision. Irene's desperation wasn't being faked. "She's just a young girl, and I'm her first love." Then: "What am I saying? She is my first love, my only love. Since before she was born she was meant for me," and he remembered the infinite sadness of the morning that brought little Irene into this world. He decided to speak to Enriqueta.

During lunch, he observed his wife's sadness. He had lived with her almost ten years and though he held affection for her, he now saw clearly that he had shared those ten years with a stranger.

Enriqueta was pretty; bending over her plate, she seemed charming, despite her sour expression. He decided to speak up.

"Enriqueta, never think that you are ugly, or that you are lost," he said, by way of introduction.

Enriqueta looked at him stonily. "Why am I going to think such stupid thoughts?" she replied, dryly.

"I don't know. Suddenly life changes, you yourself change, you realize that you've been deceived and that you've deceived others..."

Enriqueta got up with great dignity from the table, trying to cut off her husband's ill-timed confession.

"Please, I don't want to hear a speech telling me you have a lover," she said angrily. She left the dining room, holding her head high.

Miguel didn't finish eating. Everything he said came out wrong. He spent a restless afternoon, assailed by the most appalling thoughts. At night, in anguish, he went out to Irene's house instead of going to bed. He couldn't figure out what the young woman meant by her threat. "Look for my obituary in the papers!" had filled him with terror. "A childish remark, that's all, a childish remark," he repeated several times before reaching his lover's house. When he got to the gate, he rang the bell insistently. He envisioned her as on that first night, crying for someone to open the door and then jumping into his car. "She was in danger and I didn't

95

believe her," he said bitterly, while he rang the bell. No one answered his ring; and yet the lights in the house went on.

"I'm going to have to tell him the truth: admit to him that Irene doesn't live here," sighed Clementina.

"I don't have the courage. You go out and tell him," said Rosalia.

"Don't ask me to do that—" answered Clementina, already in her nightgown.

"Well, I don't know what we are going to do. We've carried this merciful lie a bit too far," her sister Rosalia answered.

"Right now I need a Turkish cigarette, like those aromatic ones father used to smoke," said Clementina, pacing.

Rosalia half-opened the door to the terrace.

"It's me, Miss Rosalia..." Miguel said, agonizing.

"What's wrong, sir?"

"I'm fine. What about her? Irene...how is she? I feel she's calling to me, looking for me, crying..."

"No, it can't be. She's fast asleep in her room. She'll call you tomorrow...It's almost daybreak now..."

"Yesterday she was so nervous...I'm afraid for her..."

Rosalia went down the steps and walked up to the gate. Miguel's wild expression frightened her.

"You're afraid of what?" she asked, scared.

"I don't know...young people are capable of anything... even of killing themselves...What an awful thought! Promise me that I will always be with her, Miss Rosalia!"

Her mouth gaped in fear.

"Promise me!" Miguel said, grabbing at the gate.

"I promise...I'll go to her." Rosalia hurried back inside the house and closed the door.

"What's wrong? You look so pale," asked her frightened sister.

"—going to commit suicide—" she stuttered.

"Stop him! Poor man!"

"Not him: Irene!" Rosalia screamed.

Both women collapsed onto a couch.

"We have to find her," Clementina urged.

"But where? If he doesn't know where she hides, how are we, two old women, going to find out?"

"This tragedy is all your fault! You were always a busybody reading too many romances! I knew this was going to end up badly, very badly," Clementina accused.

*   *   *

Miguel woke up very early. He was peaceful but felt he was a prisoner within the walls of his own house.

"The newspapers!...Where are the newspapers!" he screamed.

A servant silently brought them to him. Miguel looked through them carefully: first, the obituary listings where his friend's name did not appear. Then he read the metro section for news of crimes. He found nothing. Then political articles, but again he found nothing. He was certain that the newspaper held the key to Irene even if he could not find it. He came to the society pages. There's where he found her. She was dressed like a bride, with a serious look on her face; her hands were clasped around a small branch of orange blossoms. But it wasn't her. The young woman was Paulina and her marriage to a very wealthy industrialist was announced as the "wedding of the year." Paulina had married that imbecile named Pablo the previous night. He let the paper drop from his hands.

"Pablo...Pablo..." he repeated in disbelief.

Looking down, he again examined her tragic expression. He picked up the newspaper and dizzily left the dining room to go to Irene's house. When he got there, he angrily shook the bell and waited. He saw Aunt Rosalia coming towards him, taking little steps down the gravel path. When she was close enough, he showed her the paper.

"Look! She's gotten married. She had a different name: Paulina. Why didn't you tell me, Miss Rosalia? Why did you deceive me?...She got married yesterday...yesterday."

"Really?...Excuse me, sir, but I didn't know her name...I didn't know her...My sister and I only wanted to comfort you, you seemed so much in love, so desperate...and these young girls nowadays are terrible..."

Miguel pointed to the photographs and held on to the gate like a shipwrecked sailor. Miss Rosalia looked upon him tenderly and then at the paper.

"Oh, yes, it's young Paulina...She lives close to here, in Montes Urales. She's a good girl, a very good girl. Do you know what, sir? Her family is from good stock, but she is ruined...If you would like, I'll go this afternoon to talk to one of her nannies—you know, they tell you everything. Call me later this afternoon."

Miguel listened to her, stunned. So the old woman did know Irene, that is, Paulina.

"Yes, I'll stop by in the afternoon...Thanks..."

He did not go home. He drove around and around in his car, making crazy plans: he would go look for Irene, would force her to annul her marriage; he would get divorced, it would be a huge scandal. It didn't matter, he could not live without her. As darkness fell, he went back to Miss Rosalia's house and hopelessly rang the bell. The old woman rushed out and confidently strolled to the gate.

"It's a real shame!...A tragedy!...The young girl cried a lot before heading to church, but her mother and her sister were determined! Determined! She and her husband left for Venice; they'll come back to Mexico two months from now..."

"Two months...she cried a lot..." Miguel repeated.

He staggered away from the gate. He moved slowly, so slowly, not knowing where he was going...

The Sor Juana Inés de la Cruz
Literature Prize

In 1993 the Guadalajara International Book Fair (FIL), the Guadalajara School of Writers (SOGEM) and the French publisher Indigo/Coté-Femmes inaugurated the Sor Juana Inés de la Cruz Prize to recognize the published work of women writers. The award was named after Sor Juana since she was the first female writer of Spanish America, and her poetry, theater and journals constitute an important contribution to the literary arts the world over.

The primary objective of the prize is to bring attention to the work of a female writer in the Spanish language; all female writers who have published a novel in the previous three years are eligible.

The prize includes publication and distribution, under a standard book contract, of the winning entry in Mexico by Fondo de Cultura Económica Press and, since 1995, translation and publication in the United States by Curbstone Press. A presentation of the award is held during the Guadalajara International Book Fair, at which time the winner is presented with a commemorative bronze sculpture of Sor Juana designed by the Portuguese sculptor Gil Simoes. The winner is a featured reader in the Los Angeles Book Festival in April, sponsored by *The Los Angeles Times*.

The winner is selected in the following manner: January, guidelines are made available to the general public; May, deadline for receiving submissions; October, decision of the judges is made public; December, award's ceremony takes place during the Guadalajara International Book Fair. Contact: SOGEM, Av. Circ. Augustín Yáñez #2839, Guadalajara, 44110, JAL, Mexico.

Past winners are:
> Angelina Muniz-Huberman for *Dulcinea encantada* (Mexico: Editorial Joaquin Mortiz, 1992)
> Marcela Serrano for *Nosotros que nos queremos tanto* (Chile: Editorial Andes, 1992)
> Tatiana Lobo for *Asalto al paraiso* (Costa Rica: EDUCA, 1992)

The prize is sponsored by Tequila Sauza S.A. de C.V.; Curbstone Press, *The Los Angeles Times*, Mayor's Office of Zapopan; The Western Technological Institute for Higher Learning, Jalisco; and General Outreach Studies, University of Guadalajara.

CURBSTONE PRESS, INC.

is a non-profit publishing house dedicated to literature that reflects a commitment to social change, with an emphasis on contemporary writing from Latin America and Latino communities in the United States. Curbstone presents writers who give voice to the unheard in a language that goes beyond denunciation to celebrate, honor and teach. Curbstone builds bridges between its writers and the public – from inner-city to rural areas, colleges to community centers, children to adults. Curbstone seeks out the highest aesthetic expression of the dedication to human rights and intercultural understanding: poetry, testimonials, novels, stories, children's books.

This mission requires more than just producing books. It requires ensuring that as many people as possible know about these books and read them. To achieve this, a large portion of Curbstone's schedule is dedicated to arranging tours and programs for its authors, working with public school and university teachers to enrich curricula, reaching out to underserved audiences by donating books and conducting readings and community programs, and promoting discussion in the media. It is only through these combined efforts that literature can truly make a difference.

Curbstone Press, like all non-profit presses, depends on the support of individuals, foundations, and government agencies to bring you, the reader, works of literary merit and social significance which might not find a place in profit-driven publishing channels. Our sincere thanks to the many individuals who support this endeavor and to the following organizations, foundations and government agencies: ADCO Foundation, Witter Bynner Foundation for Poetry, Connecticut Commission on the Arts, Connecticut Arts Endowment Fund, Ford Foundation, Greater Hartford Arts Council, Junior League of Hartford, Lawson Valentine Foundation, LEF Foundation, Lila Wallace-Reader's Digest Fund, The Andrew W. Mellon Foundation, National Endowment for the Arts, the Puffin Foundation and the Samuel Rubin Foundation.

Please support Curbstone's efforts to present the diverse voices and views that make our culture richer. Tax-deductible donations can be made by check or credit card to Curbstone Press, 321 Jackson St., Willimantic, CT 06226 Tel: (860) 423-5110.